I0593526

THE NEXT BIG THING

Woods Sisters #1

ABRA PRESSLER

sugarbush press

For Percy.

You were with me every step of the way.

ACKNOWLEDGEMENT OF COUNTRY

The Next Big Thing was written on Ngunnawal and Wiradjuri land. The author pays respect to elders past and present; and acknowledges the storytelling that has taken part on these lands for millennia.

First edition published 2022

Copyright © Sugarbush Press 2022

Print ISBN: 978-0-6488043-1-4

Cover design by Kris Hack at Temys Designs

Edited: Tegan Lyon

This book is written in Australian English and some words may have alternate spellings.

This book contains coarse language, mature sexual content and 'open door' sex scenes. It is **not** suitable for younger readers.

This book, and it's e-version, are submitted to the National Library of Australia under the legal deposit scheme.

PROLOGUE

It's almost ten in the evening when Laurie calls. Her name flashes across my phone screen as I scroll through Instagram in bed. To say I hadn't expected the call is an understatement. Certainly not so soon, and certainly not so late.

I don't want to look eager, so I let it ring a few times before answering. 'Hello?'

'Hey Jordan, it's Laurie! I wanted to k—'

A passing tram drowns out Laurie's chirpy voice, its bell chiming in warning. She swears.

I press the phone against my ear and roll onto my stomach, wedging the pillow underneath my arms. 'Laurie. You still there?'

'Sorry!' she replies, almost too-loud. 'I'm walking home after a late one at the café. A BMW tried to cut off the tram.' Laurie blows out a long breath. 'Let me start over. I want to offer you the barista job... and I wanted to know if you could start tomorrow?'

Two days ago, Marco text me that his friend Laurie was looking for a barista. Good pay, flexible hours, all the coffee I could drink on shift. This couldn't have worked out better. 'Definitely. What time should I start?'

'Seven? Coffee's on the house.'

There's little I won't do for a quality-made coffee. I've been surviving off whatever instant I can scrounge from the share kitchen. 'I'll take you up on that.'

Laurie laughs. It's a laugh that turns heads; warm and inviting and a bit infectious. If ever a laugh represented someone, it's Laurie's. Before the job interview, she'd just finished making a batch of cookies, and as I'd stepped into the quaint cottage-cafe on one of the busiest streets of Melbourne, the scent of vanilla and burnt sugar had practically slapped me in the face.

'You're, like, my first real hire. I'm really looking forward to working with you.' She sounds genuine. Worry twists my stomach and I realise I don't want to disappoint her. 'Me too.'

'Okay, well, I'll see you at seven.'

'See you at seven,' I confirm.

As I hang up, I reach down for the cord of my phone charger. I plug it in and set an alarm for six.

Mattress springs squeak as someone shifts in the bunk beside me. 'Take the call outside,' they grumble, words smothered by the pillow. 'It's fucking rude.'

'Sorry,' I whisper.

I roll over. The sheets scratch against my bare legs. They smell like cheap detergent. Outside, rain pebbles against the windows. I take a deep breath in, smell the petrichor that drifts through the single cracked window on the other side of the room; earthy, muddy, relaxing. It reminds me of summer storms in Sydney; of hot days broken by evening rain. Those memories, though vivid, feel far away.

The last few months were tense. Now that I have a job, everything will get easier.

It's gotta get easier.

Someone on the other side of the dorm room snores.

Perfect.

CHAPTER ONE

I have one rule. Don't talk to me until I've had my coffee.

That was the sign my sister Erin blue-tacked to my office door last Christmas, along with a 'but first, coffee' mug as her secret Santa gift. Olivia, our social media manager, had giggled at the entire spectacle.

My love of coffee is simply that. It's a passion. An interest. A harmless vice. Living in Melbourne, one is amongst friends. It's one of the most coffee-obsessed cities and you only need to go a few blocks to find a hit.

As I sit in bumper-to-bumper traffic on a miserable Monday, my composure fraying, I'm forced to acknowledge that maybe I have a bit of a problem.

A teeny tiny caffeine addiction.

The traffic light turns green and the cars in front of me inch forward. Finally.

My best investment over lockdown was my home coffee machine. This morning, as I wrangled my stubborn, screaming four-year-old out the door, I shot espresso like a twenty-year-old throwing back tequila. Still, my caffeine addiction is rearing its ugly head. It craves real coffee. A five-dollar, Arabica-blend, oak milk flat white, specifically.

Four cars have crossed the intersection before the traffic turns amber. I let out a sigh as I stop again. Behind me, someone leans on their horn; frustrated with the brevity of the green light.

'We've all got places to be, buddy,' I grumble. 'No need to be such an asshole.'

Rain smatters over my windscreen, triggering the wipers. A text message from Erin flashes up on the screen of my Mercedes.

Got coffee. Am stalling INFLUENCE. Get here ASAP!!

I check my navigation system and nav predicts I'll arrive at the pavilion by nine-thirty but I haven't moved more than a few metres in the past five minutes.

The light turns green again, but the road is crammed. There's no way to cross without lingering in the intersection. The green light taunts me. Laughs at me. I consider risking it, inching forward and loitering in the intersection but a fine is the last thing I need this morning.

Beeeeeep! A car behind me blares. *Beeeeeep!*

I sigh and lean over my steering wheel. Fuck Mondays.

It's almost nine-thirty by the time I pull into the muddy carpark of the pavilion. Even in the awful weather, the building and the grounds are stunning. Reddish maple trees and yellow peplums line the grounds, their leaves scattered across the lush grassland.

I lock the car and walk the towards the entry to the pavilion, all the while wishing I hadn't worn my black heeled boots for the first time this year. It had finally felt cold enough to throw them on, but as I focus on not breaking my ankle on the uneven, wet terrain, I'm seriously regretting it.

'You made it.'

I glance up to see Michelle, the careers editor of INFLUENCE, standing by the entrance of the pavilion. Arms crossed and brow raised, it's clear she's not in a forgiving mood.

'Sorry, traffic was a nightmare,' I say as I shake Michelle's hand. 'Nice to finally meet face-to-face.'

'You too.' Her firm handshake takes me off-guard and I do my best not to wince. 'Come on, I'll get you set up.'

Michelle leads me through the foyer and into a large solarium. The solarium is gorgeous; lush exotic plants line the walls. Birds of paradise reach towards the glass roof, their leaves thick and glossy. Professional lights illuminate a small section of garden and people fuss with the props. Someone's wiping down the leaves to a giant elephant ear with a cloth. It's all quite surreal.

'Since you're late, we'll go ahead with Erin's solo shoot first,' Michelle says. 'Our makeup artist Eve will get started on you.'

She points to the hair and makeup station in what appears to be a storage room. Outdoor chairs rest against the wall, though Michelle has utilised two for each station. Erin sits in one chair. She's chatting with Raf, our long-time hairstylist and close friend. He's leaning over her, completely enraptured with whatever Erin's saying. It's almost a shame to interrupt them.

Erin's eyes dart to me, and she smiles. 'You got here.'

'I did.' I give Raf a kiss on the cheek. 'Good to see you, hon.'

He squeezes my shoulder as he kisses my other cheek. It's fine. He's Spanish. 'It's been too long.'

Raf's right and guilt sets in. A few years ago, we'd been inseparable—of course, we'd also been living together. Now that we lead different lives, it's harder to keep in touch. 'We'll have to arrange a regular coffee date around your overseas trips and Poppy's swimming lessons. Oh, and music lessons. Apparently if you get your pre-school aged kid proficient in an instrument, it looks good on school applications.'

That makes Erin laugh.

'You look beautiful,' I say, falling into the seat beside her. There's a coffee with my name on it beside the makeup artist's brushes. It's still warm. I take a sip and revel in the flavour. 'They will have to do some serious work on me. I only got five hours' sleep last night.'

Raf raises an eyebrow. 'Bingeing again?'

'If you mean reviewing every detail Mrs Coleman's iron-clad prenuptial, then yes,' I reply. 'Not a loophole in sight.'

Erin purses her lips. 'That poor woman. She gave her life to that man. Why did she sign such a horrendous thing?'

'To prove that she loved him,' I reply as Eve, the makeup artist, approaches. She's in her early twenties with a sweet full face, a bob of blonde hair and the most perfectly shaped eyebrows I've ever seen. Erin knows we don't talk about clients in public; so we shelve the Colette discussion for later.

Colette Coleman is a case we see too often at Grace House: women who love men so deeply and completely that they sign shitty prenuptial agreements in which they barely benefit and they're left with nothing after the divorce. Most sign it in good faith, not wanting to rock the boat or cast ill on their marriage, but the reality is fifty percent of marriages end up in divorce. While they're happily married, most women stop working, have children, and stop contributing to their superannuation funds.

Then the divorce happens, and they're left with literally nothing.

Olivia, our communications manager, developed our website's search engine optimisation content so the minute they type in the keywords 'help' and 'divorce', they're served Grace House as their first result. We try to help as many people like Mrs. Coleman get back on their feet. For many, adjusting to a new way of life is the hardest part of the divorce.

'Erin,' Michelle calls from behind. 'We're ready for you.'

Erin smooths down her pantsuit and takes a deep breath. 'God, I hope they edit these photos.'

I don't want to tell her that INFLUENCE has a strictly no Photoshop policy, but Raf squeezes her shoulder and says, 'You are beautiful, *querida*,' in that to-die-for Spanish accent and I see my sister just melt.

Raf falls into Erin's seat as Eve starts on my eye makeup.

'Raf, I hate to be that person, but could you just put the coffee in my hand?' I hear someone huff out a chuckle. I'm not sure if it's Raf or Eve, but someone places my coffee into my outstretched claw.

'You're overdue for a haircut, Miss Woods,' Raf chides.

'You're just so busy, it's impossible to book in,' I reply as Eve works colour into my eye crease.

'You know I'd move heaven and earth to fit you in if only you'd ask,' Raf replies. My hair is currently held back with a claw clip, and I know he's going to fuss and tut over it the moment that he gets his hands on it.

'I honestly don't remember the last time I cut my hair.'

'It was August last year. After much back-and-forth, I convinced you to get a trim before we washed and styled it for the Blue Foundation Gala.'

That makes sense. When I'd MC'd for a fundraising event last August, my hair had been the last thing on my mind.

'It's been almost ten months, Ana, and I hate to break it to you darling, but you're going grey.'

I gasp in mock hurt. 'Rafael, how dare you.'

Eve laughs beside me.

'It is the truth. You need to come see me more,' he says. 'We are in our thirties now, it is inevitable.'

Eve starts on my other eye and in the break, I peep to see Raf scrolling through the calendar on his phone. 'I have an opening in two weeks. A Saturday. I'm pencilling you and Poppy in.'

To be fair, Poppy could use a haircut. Plus, Raf's hair massages feel like heaven. 'Twist my arm, why don't you?'

'I know. Being pampered is so hard to schedule into your busy life.' There's absolutely no sympathy in Raf's tone, that loveable, gorgeous bastard. 'You need an assistant.'

Eve starts on my other eye as I take a sip of my coffee.

'I'm going to go watch Erin, okay?' Raf says. He looks to Eve. 'Give me a shout when you're done with makeup?'

'Will do,' Eve replies. I hear Raf's heeled loafers click against the floorboards as he goes in search of Erin.

'You're not that grey, just saying,' Eve says once Raf's out of earshot. A laugh bubbles up, making me choke on my coffee. 'A couple of strands.'

'Thank you, but I really am overdue.' If Rafael's career as a hairstylist didn't work out, he'd be a fantastic personal assistant. I've been putting it off, but perhaps Rafael's right. I do need an assistant.

Deep in my handbag, I hear my phone chime.

Eve pulls away. 'You need to get that?'

'No, it's fine.' I was already super late. I don't want to hold this photoshoot up more than I already have. Unless the office is burning down, the call can wait an hour.

I catch myself in the mirror, half-made up. Eve's chosen a cool-toned grey smoky eye, something I'd never do myself.

'The grey tones make green eyes really pop,' she says, meeting my gaze in the mirror. 'I'm thinking of a nice cool-toned red lipstick?'

I nod in agreement. 'I'll be very glamourous for my meetings this afternoon.'

Eve wears an expression I know all too well as she reaches for her lipstick palette. It's a look of boldness and fear; like she's on the precipice of a big jump.

Whatever the approach, the end question is the same. Eve dives right in.

'When INFLUENCE contracted me to do the shoot, they sent me your bio,' she says. 'I ended up on your website. My sister...,' she hesitates. 'Her boyfriend's a real asshole.'

I nod. 'I understand.'

'Do you think you could help her?'

We also get this a lot. Strangers who we meet in passing—baristas in coffee shops, people we sit beside at a gala dinner, the woman doing our makeup—they all have stories like this. One in four women has been assaulted in their lifetime. Some are still there. They're still navigating the barrage of emotions. We built Grace House for them; to give them a safe way out.

Others have left, have started over, but the trauma never leaves them. Grace House helps them too.

'We need her to make the first step,' I say. 'I can give you my card, and she can give the office a call or she can come in one day, but we can't intervene. She has to come to us.'

Once she finishes my makeup, Eve takes the card and slips it into her wallet. My card is discreetly designed. It doesn't say anything about Grace House or what we do. It looks like an appointment card, with a message to 'call Ana to reschedule' and my number underneath. One of the most dangerous times is when a woman decides to leave, and the last thing we want is a flyer that says *Domestic Violence Support Services* found by their abuser in their wallet or handbag.

'I'll talk to her. Privately,' Eve says. 'Thank you.'

The rest of the photoshoot goes smoothly. We wrap early, finishing up at just around eleven-thirty which pleases Michelle and means I get a bit of a lunch break before my meeting with Colette this afternoon.

Michelle shakes our hands but this time, I'm ready for her firm grip. Any agitation about running late has, thankfully, smoothed over. Like the rainy morning, Michelle's stern demeanour has melted into something warmer. As we step into the damp carpark of the pavilion, beams of sunshine spill onto the parkland.

'I hope to see you both at the award ceremony next month,' says Michelle. 'And I'll make sure our team sends a few copies of the printed magazine to your office.'

'Much appreciated, thank you,' Erin replies as we walk back to our cars.

It's only when I think to pull out my car keys, I remember the outstanding text on my phone. Fishing it out from the bottom of my handbag, I thumb through my list of notifications: one email from Olivia at the office, another from Greg Pryor, a landlord we rent housing through, and—

'Holy fucking shit,' I say, stopping dead in my tracks.

Erin whips around. 'What is it?'

I hand her the phone and watch as her brow furrows. 'Oh God,' she groans. 'What are you gonna do?

I read over the message again. There's no question who it's from.

Just two sentences. No greeting. No sign off. No politeness, just—*I'm in Melb next week. Want to see my daughter.*

CHAPTER TWO

My mother never used her kitchen. It was a running joke in the family. Our chef or my nanny made everything we ate. Custom birthday cakes, pizzas ordered from the local takeout shop every Friday night. The fridge was always full, but the kitchen was spotless. Any time my sisters or I tried to apply ourselves to the culinary arts, my mother would roll her eyes and complain that we were only making messes for the cleaners.

When I walk into Laurie's, it feels like how home is supposed to feel. It's quarter-to-seven in the morning, the sun barely a hint on the horizon but inside the cafe, the ovens are on and the sweet smell of baking muffins hangs in the air.

The cafe is narrow and split-level, with a sunken kitchen, coffee machine and small dining area. Golden cabinets line the top floor, each shelf displaying one of Laurie's intricately decorated cupcakes. Another cabinet displays full cakes; both for sale whole and cut into pieces.

A few steps into the sunken dining area, Laurie stands by the coffee machine, hovering over the milk-frother. She's tall; that's one of the first things you notice about Laurie. She's about six-foot with a bob of blonde hair streaked with blue. A phoenix tattoo climbs up one side of her neck.

'Coffee?' she says without looking up.

'Definitely.'

She indicates towards the office door with her head. 'Got your uniform all set out. Go get changed and the coffee will be done by the time you're ready.'

I step into the small back rooms of Laurie's café. To the right there's a tiny office space with a desk, a filing cabinet, a corkboard, and a computer. A photo of Laurie is pinned to the corkboard; she's wearing the same teal and white uniform she's got on now. Behind her, Laurie's is barely a shell of a café. An 'Opening Soon!' banner hangs from the roof.

I turn my attention to the uniform laid out on the desk. It's is something else. A pink and teal pinstripe shirt sits on the desk, along with a teal linen apron. I slip it on and to my surprise; it fits. I'm not exactly a small guy; six-foot-three and bulky. Dad always said if I put my heart into it, I'd be a decent rugby player.

I step out of the office. I've never shied away from a pink outfit—the pink linen suit I wore on New Year's Day went down treat—but I feel like I've joined a barbershop quartet.

'Looks good!' Laurie beams and hands me my coffee and we walk through her opening routine. It's straight-forward; set up the outdoor seating; open the registers, run the coffee machine.

One of her regulars lingers by the front of the shop as we set up the outdoor seating together. He's wearing a Geelong Cats beanie, but when I try to make conversation with him, he only offers me a tight smile.

'I'll make his coffee if you finish setting up,' Laurie says. I nod and she ushers the customer inside. A few minutes later, he passes me as I enter the café, the outdoor seating now set up. I give him a tight smile.

'See you again soon,' I say as I pass him, but he doesn't reply.

'Michael's non-verbal,' Laurie explains as she wipes down the milk-frother with a wet rag. 'He comes through most mornings for a latte, one sugar. Always pays with cash.'

Laurie leads me to the cramped back office.

'I'll introduce you to our other regulars as they come through,' she says as she shows me through the walk-in-fridge and the way she's specifically organised milk. She grabs a milk carton and hands it to me. 'We restock our working fridges every night; I had a custom order last night, so I skipped it. I have a heap of orders today, so I'll get you to handle the coffee machine, okay?'

'Okay,' I reply, desperate to project confidence. While I have a barista qualification, these are the only coffees I've ever made. I may have massaged my resume a bit, but when you're down to your last hundred dollars, you gotta tell some white lies. After a couple of customers leave without complaint, I figure I must not be too bad.

A woman comes in, but before I greet her, Laurie sees her over my shoulder. She emerges from the kitchen with an enormous chocolate cake. It's covered in shiny ganache and has the words 'happy birthday, Mark' written in white icing. I've no clue who Mark is, but I wanna go to this party for the cake.

The woman pays, takes her cake and Laurie goes back into the kitchen. 'Wow, it's great having you here.' She laughs. 'I'm so productive!'

Within the next hour, Laurie creates two small works of art: a gorgeous golden sponge cake with fresh cream and strawberries and a Tim-Tam cheesecake she prepared the night before. She slides both into the cake cabinet.

At eleven, we break for another coffee. At least, Laurie does. Her face is flushed red from the heat of the kitchen, her hair slightly frizzy around the roots.

'Not bad,' she says as she takes a sip of my coffee. 'Do you feel comfortable running the place for a few hours this afternoon? You seem to have a handle on things, and I finished my cake orders. It'd just be nice to get some laundry done. I'll be back to close about three.'

'That's fine.' I feel like it's very much not fine. What if something happens? What if I get robbed?

I can't believe Laurie's been running the cafe on her own for so long. Not only is it unsafe, but the cafe is incredibly busy. Since opening, we've enjoyed a steady stream of customers. Most stick around for a yarn and Laurie's happy to oblige. She oozes charisma; she remembers names, orders, and the little things like a customer's kid's soccer game.

Around eleven-thirty, two women walk into the cafe. It's impossible not to notice them; one wears a black fitted suit, her dark hair slicked into a low bun. She's all business. The other woman is blonde, ringlets of platinum hair cascade down her shoulders and back. I recognise her cream woollen jumper from last year's Chanel Autumn-Winter release. My mother has the same one.

The businesswoman gives me a small smile as they approach the counter. I grab a few menus and go to greet them.

'Ana!' Laurie calls from the kitchen. She wipes her soapy hands on a tea towel as she emerges. Ana must be one of the regulars. 'How's things?'

'Good,' she replies. Her dark eyes flick to me. 'Who's this? A new hire!'

'He is!' Laurie spins towards me. 'This is Jordan, my new café all-rounder. Jordan, this is Ana. She works down the road.'

'Nice to meet you. It's my first day,' I explain.

'But his coffee is excellent,' Laurie replies as she leads Ana and her friend to a table in the back corner.

I give them a few minutes to get settled and I finish wiping down the top of the coffee machine before grabbing my order pad.

As I approach, the blonde woman has removed her sunglasses. Deep dark circles hang under her puffy eyes. Clearly, she's going through something. I focus on Ana and plaster on a smile. 'What can I get you both?'

Ana looks to her friend, who takes the lead. 'Chai latte, but with like, half a shot of coffee.'

Weird order, but okay. I look at Ana.

'Flat white, skim milk with one sugar.' She picks up the menu to scan. 'And a slice of strawberry cream sponge cake, please?' She turns back to her friend. 'I think this situation calls for a bit of cake, don't you think?'

The other woman nods. Whatever's going on in her life, it's clearly not great. Ana hands me both menus. 'Thank you, Jordan.'

Something runs through me. Maybe it's the shock

of her saying my name in her honeyed tones. It's hypnotising. Like the people who narrate sleep stories; or do late-night radio. Or maybe it's the simple fact that she remembered it; took notice of it. Took notice of me.

I clear my throat. 'Be back soon.'

'Thank you.' Her dark eyes flash. Somehow, I know she's always gotta have the last word.

Laurie's washing dishes in the kitchen, so I make the coffee before plating a slice of the sponge cake. As I load the order onto the serving tray, nerves set in. I've never used a serving tray before. I've run most of the orders myself. Lifting the tray, my arm shakes. It's not heavy at all, but the tray feels unbalanced; feels wrong.

I glance up. Though it's barely ten steps, Ana's table feels very far away.

I take a tentative step forward, find my balance. Find my confidence. Then I go for it. I don't give myself time to overthink and stride across the cafe floor towards Ana's table.

Big mistake.

Out of the corner of my eye, I see a girl rush behind me as she runs towards someone entering the cafe. Her foot kicks the back of mine. It's barely a tap but it's enough to feel it. I lose focus. I lose balance.

As I fall backwards, I try to rebalance myself, but all I do is overcompensate. The coffees lurch and someone screams. I'm falling for real and everything I'm carrying is about to end up in Ana's lap.

Desperately, I try to regain control of the serving tray. I pull it backwards and feel hot coffee splash against my chest, down my arms.

A glass falls to the tiles and shatters. My knees hit

the ground first and I drop the tray on instinct as my hands push out to catch my fall.

Sometimes, instinct bites you in the arse.

A hot stab of pain shoots up my arm. Blood oozes into the coffee puddle. I'm surrounded by shards of glass and every movement just embeds whatever's already in me a bit deeper. I'm considering how to get off my hands and knees when hands hook under my armpits. They haul me backwards, dragging me across the tiles until I'm sitting on my ass.

Ana kneels beside me and grabs my wrists. 'Let me see your hands,' she demands. Slowly, she turns my palm over. 'Oh shit.'

'Press a napkin onto it while I get the first aid kit,' Laurie instructs. Ana takes the napkins and presses them to my palms. Instantly, blood seeps through the thick paper.

The blonde woman steps over a puddle of coffee, glass and blood to kneel in front of me. 'He's going to need stitches. We should call an ambulance.'

Shit. Ambulance rides were not the plan for today. They're also not a health service included on Medicare.

Thankfully, Ana replies, 'It would be quicker to drive him. My car is just around the block.' She packs more napkins onto my hand as Laurie returns with the first aid kit. Another customer places paper towels over the spill.

Ana grabs her handbag as Laurie helps me stand. 'I'm taking him to hospital.'

'I'm so sorry,' I mutter. Just the act of standing makes my head spin. I close my eyes and will it to pass.

'Accidents happen, it's fine,' she says though I can tell it definitely isn't fine. I know she'd been looking forward to her break this afternoon; looking forward to having an extra hand around the cafe.

I just had to go slice mine open.

So much for the job.

CHAPTER THREE

The Royal Prince Alfred Hospital is only a few kilometres away, but with the rain coming down in sheets outside, and ambulances spread across the district, it'll be easier to drive the barista to the hospital than wait for one to show up.

As I grab my handbag, Laurie helps Jordan stand. The guy's built like a rugby player; tall with shoulders wide enough to fill a doorframe. Laurie hooks her shoulder under his and heaves him up. He stumbles to his feet, clutching at his bleeding hand. Colette's dressed it, but without stitches, it's going to bleed straight through.

I touch his shoulder. 'Can you walk?'

Jordan nods. 'I think so.'

I grasp Jordan's arm as Laurie steps away. She gives me a tight smile. 'Thank you, Ana. Really.'

'It's fine,' I assure her. I feel awful leaving the cafe in such a state, but Jordan needs to get to the hospital. He takes a hesitant step forward and doesn't fall flat on his face, so with a little support, we make our way out of the cafe and onto the wet street. Colette holds the umbrella over our heads as we walk towards my car.

'Oh God.' Jordan stops at the curb as I unlock the car. 'I don't want to bleed all over your Mercedes.'

We don't have time for this. 'It'll be fine,' I reply. 'I have a kid. It's seen its fair share of fluids.' I ease him into the car, police-style. 'Watch your head.'

I start up the engine as Jordan looks around the interior. He clocks the booster seat in the back row. 'It's nice.'

'Thanks,' I reply as I drive down the narrow side-street and slip onto the main road. It's the middle of the day; traffic is sparser than usual, but the rain slows us down. We stop at a red light; the silence almost unbearable. 'How about some music?'

Jordan nods. I put on the first radio station the radio picks up, not bothering to connect my phone. Somehow, I don't think he'd vibe the Frozen sound-track that seems to dominate my Spotify.

'You feeling okay?' I ask as we wait at the longest red light in history. Blood is seeping through his bandage despite the pressure, and he looks a little green around the gills. Not good. 'We're almost at the hospital.'

Jordan licks his lips. Says something I don't catch. The light turns green.

'Sorry, what was that, hon?' It's hard to focus on the road and on the kid having a breakdown in my passenger seat.

'I said, what if I can't play?'

'I'm sure the team will understand.' The lights to the Prince Alfred Hospital come into view just as I catch another red light. 'It'll be okay. A few stitches and you'll be right as rain.'

'Not the team. I meant the guitar.' His voice breaks. I don't dare look him in the eye to see if he's crying or not. 'It's like my entire thing.'

I focus on the red light, willing it to turn. When I woke up this morning, I didn't expect to have someone crying in the front seat of my car. If Erin was here, she'd know what to say. What to do. She's good with people and their emotions. I keep my eyes fixed on the light as Jordan wipes his nose on the sleeve of his uniform.

The light turns green.

We turn into the parking bay and make our way into the emergency department. Jordan clutches his bleeding hand as we check in. The last time I was in the hospital, I was pushing out a baby, but the sickly sweet smell of the disinfectant is always the same.

A handful of people are already waiting in the emergency room when we arrive. The nurse directs us to sit on the plastic seats and fill out a clipboard of forms as she calls another ER nurse. Once we take a seat, I flick through the paperwork.

'Middle name?' I grab the pen attached to the clipboard.

'Um, Anthony,' Jordan replies. He looks down at his converses. They're well-worn and faded black.

'Last name?' I prompt.

Jordan doesn't reply. He tries to flex the fingers of his bad hand, but just winces.

'Don't do that,' I chide. 'Last name?'

'Templeton.' It's more of a grumble than an answer.

'Templeton?' I echo.

'Yeah. T-e-m-,'

'I know how to spell Templeton.' I put the form down and turn to look at him. 'You're a Templeton?'

Jordan avoids my eye and shrugs. 'It's not a big deal.'

The Templetons are only one of the most influential families in Sydney, and, by extension, Australia. 'Your dad's Anthony Templeton?'

'Unfortunately.'

Anthony was a pro rugby player who, after retirement, made his fortune in property development. I see Jordan's resemblance to Anthony now; blue eyes, high cheekbones, curly blonde hair. Explains the rugby shoulders, too.

'What else do you need to know?' Jordan motions to the paperwork with his good hand.

I look down. 'Date of birth?'

'First of February 2002.'

I scribble it down. 'We're ten years apart,' I note. 'Address?'

'Just put Laurie's place.'

My pen hovers on the paper. 'Why? You don't live there.'

Jordan grabs at his hand. 'Where's the doctor? I think I'm bleeding through the bandage.'

'I have to put down an address,' I say. 'Should I write your place in Syd-,'

'No,' Jordan snaps. I can tell he's debating telling me the answer. '102 Little Lonsdale Street. In the city.'

I recognise the address. 'You're living at the Youth Hostel?'

Jordan keeps his eyes fixed on the ground. 'It's not like it's permanent. Just until I get back on my feet.'

'I'm not judging you.' I wonder if his father knows he's living in a youth hostel? Based on the way he'd reacted when I mentioned his father, I'd guess not. I jot down an address.

Jordan realises what I'm doing. 'That's not—'

'I know. It's my address.' Technically, it's Grace House's address. I hand him the form to sign. 'How did you end up at the youth hostel?'

'I don't want to get into it now, if you don't mind,' he says firmly as he scribbles his signature. I take it back to the office desk, and then wait a little longer before we're called into the consultation rooms.

'Did a number on this one, didn't you?' the nurse jokes as she unravels the soiled bandage. 'Doesn't seem to be too deep. We'll wash it out and give you a few stitches.'

'Stitches,' Jordan mutters. I reach forward and grab his good hand, squeezing his icy fingers. He gives me a weak smile.

'Thanks for staying,' he says.

'No worries,' I reply.

'You're late,' Erin calls from the kitchen as I step into my apartment. Poppy's backpack hangs on the hook of the door. 'I've got the vodka in the freezer. Kid's fed and in bed.'

I toe off my shoes and throw my handbag over the back of the lounge before joining my sister in the kitchen. She's barefoot, pouring vodka into a cocktail shaker. Two martini glasses sit on the countertop. 'Thanks for picking Pops up from school. We were at the hospital longer than I thought.'

Erin pours the espresso martinis and slides one across the bench top. 'So what happened? You were incoherent on the phone.'

'The barista tripped and fell at Laurie's. Sliced his

hand open. I took him to the hospital and stayed with him until they stitched him up, then I dropped him home.' I don't tell Erin that his home was a youth hostel in the city. The fewer details, the better.

'Poor kid,' Erin laments as she sips on her cocktail. 'Anyway, here's the cherry on the sundae of your shitty day.' She pauses for emphasis. I truly believe my sister finds pleasure in the dramatics of my life. 'Jon called the office today.'

'Great. What did he want?'

'To talk to you,' Erin replies smugly. 'He didn't leave a message with Olivia.'

Jon only messaged me this morning. After almost five years of hearing diddly squat, it's pretty rich to be following up a text message within twelve hours.

I take my martini and wave Erin over to the lounge. It's one of my favourite parts of this apartment: slightly sunken with a small electric fireplace and a large television. With the blinds closed and the fire going, curling up on my plush modular lounge is like being transported to a log cabin in the Dandenongs.

Erin sits beside me, tucking her feet under her bottom and resting her arm on the back of the lounge. 'You're not considering it, are you?'

'Romantically? Not in a million years,' I reply. 'But he is Poppy's dad. It's the first genuine effort he's made in four years.'

'Exactly,' Erin replies. 'He's taken four years to reach out. Why? What does he want from you now?'

It's a fair question. When we were together, we weren't rich. While I'm definitely not rich now, I have built a better life for myself and our daughter in the years since. I don't know what Jon's been up to. Maybe he's worked on himself. God, I hope so.

'I'm still angry at him,' Erin admits over the lip of her martini glass. 'Like, so fucking angry at him. I haven't forgiven him for any of what he put you through.'

'Neither have I.' I feel like I have to defend myself. Sometimes Erin can get on her high horse a bit. This feels like one of those times. 'We still have massive issues, but if he wants a relationship with his daughter, I'd be the shitty parent if I didn't let him.'

'But he's putting you in that position again!' she replies quickly. Erin takes a breath, takes a sip of her martini and calms herself down. 'Well, speaking of Jon, how is your love life?'

We see each other every day at work and most weekends. She knows there's been no one in my life for years, and yet she asks me if I'm seeing anyone almost every other week. Like I have some secret boyfriend and we've been having secret dates in the lucrative spare time I have between putting Poppy to bed and my 5am workout.

'Non-existent. Yours?'

Erin shrugs, which just makes me more suspicious. I didn't think she was seeing anyone, but I've missed things when I'm stressed. 'Spill.'

She pouts over the lip of her glass. 'Ed's back.'

'You're joking.' Have I missed a memo or are we being tormented by the ghosts of boyfriends past? What kid do I have to be nice to in order to break this fucking curse?

'No,' she laments, sinking into the back of the couch. 'And it gets worse. He's single.'

That is bad news. 'Didn't he get engaged to that other woman; the doctor?'

The doctor Ed left Erin for; the doctor he'd met

mere weeks before he flew to work for Doctors Without Borders.

Erin nods. 'They broke it off, and he left his post to go backpacking in Europe. He got back last month.'

'That's a lot of information to know about someone you haven't spoken to in three years.' Erin's gaze drifts away from mine. At least she has the gall to look guilty. 'Erin.'

'In my defence, he messaged me first.'

I scoff. 'You can't be thinking about it?'

Erin looks down into her almost empty martini glass and swishes the liquid around. Clearly, she has been thinking about it. 'We just got coffee. It was fine.'

God, it's worse than I thought. They got coffee.

'It was nice to catch up with him,' she adds. 'But my feelings for him are gone. As soon as I saw him, I felt bad about myself. You know, how I used to feel.'

In our early twenties, Ed was gaslighting Erin before we even knew what it was. I'd had my own issues with Jon and Erin's relationship had seemed so perfect on paper. Ed was a newly minted doctor. He'd helped us find a placement in a nursing home for our Mum. He'd walk Poppy around the block when she cried while we were out for coffee. So when one of Erin's friends found his secret dating profile, he'd convinced her a catfish had stolen his identity. We'd believed him.

'Anyway, he said he wants to refer patients from his new practice to Grace House,' Erin finishes. 'What do you think?'

I don't want Ed anywhere near my life or my business, but I don't have that luxury. Why does it feel like my back's against the wall? Ed knows I can't turn him away. Not from an ethical standpoint; and not without sacrificing my reputation.

'You don't have to say it's a bad idea. It's written all over your face,' Erin says and downs the rest of her martini.

CHAPTER FOUR

'Please.' I put my hand on the counter to emphasise the bandages. The hostel receptionist, an older woman with frizzy red hair, regards me with a haughty expression. There's not an ounce of sympathy in her gaze. 'I swear I'll settle once my pay comes through. Just one more night.'

The receptionist crosses her arms. 'A night you can't pay for.'

'I'll pay it back and the next fortnight in advance.' The meagre earnings I made from my one shift at Laurie's will barely cover a few nights' board, but I'm not telling her that.

She shakes her head. 'No money, no board.'

'Come on,' I implore, leaning over the counter. 'Just one more night.'

Outside, the wind whips against the door. Surely she won't kick out a guy with eight stitches in his hand? Not in this weather.

'Please,' I beg. I'm not above begging now. But just as I notice her expression soften, my mouth goes and ruins it. 'Isn't there someone else I can talk to? The manager?'

As soon as I say it, I know I'm done for. Might as well pack my bags. The receptionist turns back to me; her cheeks flushed and her mouth a long white line.

'I *am* the manager,' she replies. 'And this isn't a homeless shelter; that's two blocks down the road. Make yourself familiar with it.' She turns back to her computer and begins typing, clearly done with this conversation. 'Be out by midday or I will donate your stuff to charity.'

Everything I have fits into a duffel bag. I'm not sure if it is incredibly economic or incredibly depressing. I throw on an extra jacket, giving the manager a final dirty look as I zip it up and brave the cold Melbourne day. Striding forward, I wrench open the front door.

Immediately, I regret it.

A spittle of rain smacks me in the face as the wind whips against my jacket. A tram skims past me, its bell ringing as it stops to let passengers off. Throwing my bag over my shoulder, I march towards the only warm spot I know; the library. I'm not expected at Laurie's until 11am, so I can squeeze in a bit of study.

The stitches came out yesterday, a week after the accident, and I've been able to play the guitar. My hand still feels tight on the piano but it'll get better with practise. Music has always been my outlet. I've always turned to it when things get tough. It's been hard not being able to play; not having that escape.

The library is a symphony of tiny noises: the tapping of keyboards, the sound of someone rifling through their backpack, and the gentle footfalls of people as they wander the halls. I find a public computer in the library and wait as it boots up.

Sunlight filters through the stained glass windows, and dust dances in a beam that lands directly beside me. Guess it must have stopped raining. Typical Melbourne.

After submitting an assignment, I grab a two-dollar sandwich from a convenience store and catch the 72 tram to Commercial Road. It takes eighteen minutes for the tram to rattle its way down to South Yarra. I find a spot to stand and gaze out the window; oak trees shed yellow and red across the wide streets, in their final, stunning performance of the season.

I ring the bell to stop as we approach Commercial Road. There's no dedicated tram stop this far out of the city. The stop is just a sign on the side of the road and one disembarks with a silent prayer that cars in the left lane won't bowl you over the second you step out. With my luck, I'm surprised it hasn't happened already. I help a woman with a pram off the tram, give a wave to a BMW driver as thanks for their patience and continue on my way.

There's a small public book exchange nestled between a hairdresser and a cafe near the tram stop in Prahran, so I swap my copy of *Catcher in the Rye* for *The Dry* and continue to Laurie's.

It's my first shift back since the incident. To say I'm nervous is an understatement. The moment I step into the cafe, my stomach lurches and it feels like I'm going to shit my pants.

Laurie glances up from the coffee machine, a smile gracing her face. 'Show us your wicked scar, then.'

I descend the stairs to show her my palm and the red two-inch jagged scar. It doesn't hurt anymore, but it gets mad itchy.

'Oh God,' Laurie says. 'I'm so sorry.'

I shrug it off. 'It was an accident. Thanks for getting workplace comp onto it so quickly.'

Not that they've done anything about the situation, mind you. It takes weeks for them to process a compensation payout for lost wages and medical bills. I practically had to beg my doctor to give me permission to return to work or face an overdrawn bank account.

Laurie slides a coffee towards me as I fasten my apron. 'Ana said she'll come in to see you tomorrow. She was really worried.'

'Oh,' I say and immediately feel like a bit of a fool. She'd stayed with me as they stitched me up and dropped me off at the hostel afterwards. I'd thought we'd run into each other eventually once I came back to work. I hadn't thought she'd ask after me. To know she was thinking about me, that I was on her mind long enough for her to ask Laurie about me, it makes me feel strange. It's the kind of feeling that should have a German name. Like *schadenfreude*.

It's a quiet afternoon. I spend the shift making coffee or cleaning. Laurie won't let me do any heavy lifting, so I'm forced to watch as she drags in the umbrellas and outdoor furniture before closing.

'I don't know why we bother having outdoor tables,' she huffs, red-faced and sweaty. 'I'm over the rain.'

I grab an umbrella out of the stand as Laurie turns off the lights. 'I think it's a La Niña year.'

She hums in annoyance as she locks the door. The sun's gone down, and this side of Chapel Street is quiet on a Thursday evening. 'You gonna be okay to get home?'

'The tram isn't too far away,' I say, glancing down

the road. I can't see headlights on the track, but the runs past often enough that Laurie nods.

'Well, stay dry. See you tomorrow.' She gives me a tight smile and then heads off down the road, car keys in her fist. Chapel Street is pretty safe, but still, I wonder if I should offer to walk her to her car. Just in case.

By the time I think about it, Laurie's disappeared.

I find refuge under the awning of an expensive shoe shop and dig my phone out from my pocket to check the timing of the next tram.

Twenty-two minutes.

Great. Must have just missed one.

I lean back on the brickwork, resolving to get comfortable and wait. If I had money, I'd grab a burger from Maccas down the road and wait there. At least it'd be dry.

As if I've offended the universe, a streak of lightning slices across a sky. Barely a breath later, thunder rumbles, strong enough to shake the window behind me. I zip up my jacket and plaster myself against the wall.

Rain falls off the awning, slapping on the pavement, and another flash of lightning lights up the sky. A Nissan with red 'P' plates careens down the street, tyres screeching as he comes to a stop by a sudden red light. He's not going fast enough to splash me, but the excess water flows up onto the pavement and soaks through my converses.

I'm excited to add athlete's foot to the ailments I've suffered this year.

Just as I go to check the app again, a car pulls over and stops in front of me. A sleek black Mercedes with tinted windows. My immediate thought is *cop*. It's not unlike coppers to do a 'welfare check' on kids loitering on the street, and the Mercedes is giving strong unmarked patrol car vibes. I pull out my phone to check the app, if only to make it seem like I'm waiting on a tram.

Which I am.

The window of the Mercedes winds down.

Shit. I'm in trouble now. There's no way my dad won't hear of this. I dunno what's worse. Being detained or facing my dad.

'Hey Jordan!' a woman calls from inside the car.

I know that voice. I push off the wall and approach the Mercedes, shading my face from the rain. Resting my elbows on the car door, I lean over.

'Ana?'

'It is you!' Ana says. She's dressed in a navy suit, her long dark hair pulled back into a low ponytail. 'What are you doing out so late?'

I feel the rain beating against my back. 'Just finished work. What are *you* doing out so late?'

'Just finished work,' she echoes. 'You wanna ride?'

Fuck yes, I do. 'You're sure?'

Ana raises an eyebrow. 'You'd prefer waiting in the rain?'

'Touché.' I open the car door and slip into the passenger seat. For a second, I worry about the rain on my clothes, but then I remember Ana telling me not to worry about getting blood on the upholstery. Surely a little water is no big deal.

Ana's car smells like leather and eucalyptus cleaning solution. It's immaculate. Soft indie music plays through the speaker system, which is hooked up to her phone. Didn't notice it the first time I was in here.

'You're the last person I expected to see out,' I say as she pulls back onto the road.

'A client meeting ran late,' she says. 'Where to?'

'City, please. Central station.'

'Back to the hostel?' she asks. There's no malice or ridicule in her tone, but I'm already on the defensive.

I scoff before I can help it. 'They kicked me out.'

Ana turns to me. 'Kicked you out?'

'I couldn't afford to stay there. But it's fine, my pay is coming in tomorrow and I'm working it out, really—'

'So where were you planning to go in the city?' Ana cuts me off.

I huff and sink further down in my seat. I'm exhausted, and it feels like my emotions are just simmering at the surface, far too close for comfort. 'Just... just somewhere I could bunk down safely for the night,' I manage. 'Like a shelter or something. I have work again in the morning and I get paid tomorrow. It's really not that big of a deal.'

We've stopped at a red light, the colour reflecting off the slick, wet road.

'You can stay with me tonight,' Ana says into the darkness.

That makes me sit up straight. 'What? No.'

The light turns green. Ana drives.

'Really, Ana, it's okay,' I say. 'Drop me off here. I'll find somewhere.'

'It's wet and late,' she replies sternly, and I know there's no use arguing with her. 'The homeless shelters will all be full. I won't let you stay out on the streets, Jordan.'

'I'm not really homeless,' I say, but Ana focuses on the road. End of conversation. I'm crashing at her place, whether I like it or not.

Ana lives in Bentleigh, a suburb south of Chapel Street. We pull into a modern apartment complex just off the main road. Ana directs me through the garage and to the lift. I press the button and we wait, bathed in the yellowish beams of the security light. The light plays on her features. She's beautiful in a haunting way, bone structure strong and precise with a square jawline and a slim curved nose. She tends to purse her lips when she focuses, like now, as the doors to the elevator open.

Ana swipes her card and hits the top floor.

Penthouse.

Fancy.

The lift ride is silent. I'd be lying if I said it wasn't awkward. I just dunno what to say to break the tension. When the elevator doors open, I almost breathe a sigh of relief. But then Ana stops me, her hand on my chest.

It takes a moment for her to realise what she's done; that she's touching me. She clears her throat. 'I just wanted to tell you before we go in...I have a cat.'

It comes out like the most sinister of secrets.

'A cat?' I echo.

Ana nods. 'A cat. You're not allergic, are you?'

'No.'

Ana unlocks the door with a knowing smile. 'Great, 'cause she's gonna love you.'

As soon as the door opens, a tortoise-shell cat barrels into the hallway. Ana lets out a long-suffering sigh and scoops the mass of fur into her arms. The cat screeches and wiggles out of her embrace, darting back into the apartment. Ana flicks on the lights and beckons me inside.

'She's a lot,' she says as she drops her handbag on

the stand by the door. 'Don't be surprised if she curls up next to you tonight.'

Sounds tempting. 'What's her name?'

'Mouse.' Ana hangs up her blazer on the coat rack and waves for me to follow her. We walk past a sunken lounge room with a plush-looking modular sofa and a TV mounted above the fireplace. It's gorgeous and probably worth a mint. I try to think back on what Ana told me she did for a living at the hospital, but it's a blur of pain and drugs.

'I found her in the alleyway catching mice after work one night,' Ana continues. 'Took her home thinking I'd give her to the RSPCA. Ended up keeping her.'

Mouse weaves between Ana's legs as she places her food bowl into the small laundry that leads off the kitchen. 'Beer?' she calls from inside.

'That'd be great, thanks.'

I shrug off my soaked jacket and place it on the back of a kitchen stool. Ana reappears from the laundry and sets two bottles of beer on the counter. 'Have you had dinner?'

'Yeah,' I lie.

'Well, I'm ordering pizza,' she replies. I dunno if Ana can tell I'm lying, or if she just doesn't care. 'Are you a fan of pineapple?'

'Big fan,' I reply as I take a sip of beer. It tastes good. I don't remember the last time I had a drink; January at least.

'Not going to win friends with that opinion,' Ana says as she grabs her credit card from her wallet.

'It's the perfect contrast to the flavours,' I argue. 'Sweet and tangy!'

'Pizza sans pineapple will be twenty minutes.' As

she takes a sip of her beer, Ana raises a single brow. 'Can I interest you in a hot shower in the meantime?'

Beer hits the back of my throat and surges up my nose. Desperately, I try not to cough, but the burn is overwhelming. A hot shower sounds divine, but I hadn't expected it to sound so suggestive.

Ana disappears into the laundry room to grab a large, fluffy towel, a pair of grey track pants and a cotton t-shirt. 'These were my ex's. You can have them.'

Wonder what happened to the ex, but no way I'm gonna ask.

'I don't have a spare room, but you can crash on the couch. The cat will probably join you.'

'A cuddle buddy,' I reply.

'More like a bed hog,' Ana laughs. 'The bathroom is down the hallway; first door on the left.'

I find my way to the bathroom, strip off and jump in the shower. At the hostel, we get two minute bursts of hot water per session. It's an equity thing; to make sure everyone gets a hot shower, but it's barely enough time to get warm, let alone wash anything important. Take longer than two minutes and you're showering cold.

Ana, on the other hand, has two shower heads.

I turn both of them on. Because why the shit not?

Hot water rushes over me; a waterfall of warmth. For a long time, I just stand in the never-ending stream. My body aches more than I thought it did; the muscles in my shoulders feel tight and hard. I wash my hair with a citrus-smelling shampoo. My dick twitches, half-hard in the stream of warm water. I don't blame it. I'm half tempted to take care of business—I don't remember the last time I had a wank—but it'd be super inappropriate.

I emerge from the bathroom, clad in Ana's ex's hoodie and track pants. I'm warm, cosy and absolutely, completely dog-tired.

'Pizza's here,' Ana says from the dining table. Behind her, Melbourne twinkles, the city's glow blurry through the haze of rain. She's changed into a pair of loose pants and a Nirvana t-shirt, her long dark hair falling over her shoulder. Ana's a beautiful woman, whether she's wearing a business suit or cradling a half-drunk beer and a slice of pizza.

I take a seat beside her, suddenly ravenous.

'I want to introduce you to my sister, Erin,' Ana says as I take a bite of pizza. She's looking at me in a way I can't quite decipher, but I'm not sure I like. 'I think she could help you out.'

I wake to the sharp sensations of Mouse's claws as she makes biscuits beside my leg. Groaning, I roll over and adjust my boxers.

'Not nice, Mouse,' I say as I grab my phone from the side table. The screen lights up. It's just after seven in the morning. There's a text from Laurie. I must have missed it last night.

Hope you got home safe.

Sure did, I type back quickly. There's no way in hell I'm telling her I ended up crashing on the couch of one of her dearest customers.

Keeping good relations with the regulars is of the utmost importance to Laurie and if she knew I'd mixed personal and professional, she'd flip. Besides, it's not like this is a recurring thing. Purely a once-off. As soon as the money comes through, I'll find a place.

As I sit up, I wonder what would have happened if Ana had been a cop last night. A Templeton skulking around the streets of Melbourne with no fixed address would definitely make the news headlines. And fuck me if I could be an even bigger disappointment to dad. He'd have nipped the story in the bud with an undisclosed amount of money and forced me on a plane back to Sydney. After that, I shudder to think.

Life might be rough, but at least I'm not under dad's thumb anymore.

The building pipes groan. I assume Ana's in the shower and then, predictably, my mind spirals into filth. Grabbing my clothes from my duffel bag, I change out of Ana's ex's hoodie and leave it on top of her washing machine.

'Hey you,' Ana says as she walks into the kitchen towelling her long hair. She's wearing a black knit dress with an oversized camel blazer. She tosses the towel on the back of a kitchen chair, letting her hair hang in damp ringlets. 'Did you sleep well?'

Somehow, seeing her like this feels wrong. Too intimate. I've never thought about seeing Ana bare-faced and freshly showered, but now I have. It feels special.

'I did, yeah,' I say.

She turns on the coffee machine. 'Coffee?'

''That'd be great,' I reply. 'Thanks. Can I use the bathroom?'

She pulls two mugs from the cupboard. 'Of course, you don't need to ask.'

In the morning light, I get a better read of Ana's apartment. Last night, sleep-deprived and out of my element, it had felt like a rabbit's warren, all dark corridors, and closed doors. Now I've got my wits about me again. It feels more manageable. There's the large living and kitchen space, with its floor-to-ceiling windows. To the right of the doorway, a narrow hallway leads to Ana's bedroom, its door slightly ajar, the main bathroom, small study nook, and another room.

With the low light and the high walls, this side of the apartment feels strangely cramped. It reminds me of Dad talking about his apartment complexes, and how he'd fit a bedroom, bathroom, and kitchen within thirty-three square metres. 'The shit these people let me get away with,' he'd said when the building was approved.

After relieving myself, I wet my hair and try to tame my curls. They're frizzy and misshapen from the wash last night, but I manage to get them under control. My uniform sits beside the sink, folded and fresh. Ana must have washed it last night.

When I return, Ana's making toast in the kitchen and a hot coffee rests on the servery. Steam curls from the mug and as I grab it, I breathe in deeply. God, I love the smell of coffee.

'I should probably head out,' I say as I take a sip. 'Thanks so much for letting me crash.'

Ana glares at me from over her shoulder. 'You're not going anywhere without breakfast.' She slides a plate of toast across the kitchen bench.

'It's fine. I normally don't eat breakfast.' I find my discarded shoes under the lounge. 'Really. You've probably got work. I don't want to overstay my welcome.'

'Jordan,' Ana says sternly, and a thrill runs through me at the tone. 'I'm not letting you out of here without breakfast.' I drop the shoe. Am I really arguing over a couple of pieces of free toast?

'Fine. Twist my arm, why don't you?'

She smiles as I take a seat at the kitchen counter. 'So, peanut butter or Vegemite?'

'Vegemite. Is that even a question?'

She hands me the jar, and I spread it on my toast. Underneath the table, Mouse rubs against my legs, mewling.

'She likes you,' Ana says as she sips her coffee. 'I told you she would.'

I take a bite of the toast. 'Must be something about me.'

Ana smiles over the lip of her mug. 'Must.'

I lean down and give Mouse a scratch under the chin.

'So, it turns out my sister can't meet you this morning,' Ana says, changing the subject, as the toaster pops again. 'You'll just have to make an appointment during the week. She can help you apply for income support and find a place to stay permanently.'

Ana must read the hesitation on my face. My sister, the politician, always told me I had a weak face. A face that wears emotions too freely. She's said I'd need to work on it if I was serious about pursuing a career in politics or law.

'I'm not doing this out of pity, Jordan,' Ana continues. 'Come into Grace House during the week and we'll talk about how we can make things easier for you. What do you have to lose?'

You're already at rock bottom, my mind adds. Still, easier would be nice. I've never asked for help from anyone. When I left Sydney with my tail between my legs, I resolved it would be the last time I took a handout from anyone.

But Ana isn't giving me a handout, I remind myself.

She's offering a leg up.

'What do you do at Grace House?' I ask.

'I'm an accountant,' she replies. Whatever I thought she was gonna say, I was not expecting that.

Surprise must be clear on my face because she smiles. 'Not what you thought I did?'

'Thought you were a lawyer. Or a CEO. An accountant is cool, but I've never seen an accountant look... well, look like you?' And in case Ana takes it the wrong way, I quickly add, 'I mean, you're pretty ripped. Not that you're not, you know, gorgeous and feminine, but I was more talking about...' My hands move up and down, referencing Ana's body, and dear God, what is wrong with me? I simply cannot shut up.

Ana just laughs. 'I started weightlifting in my second year of university. Accounting is...' she pauses, searching for the right word. 'Hard. Lots of thinking. It was nice to focus on my body. Calming. When I'm working out, I only need to focus on one thing.'

I can understand that. When I'm playing, all I focus on is the notes. Music drowns out all other noise.

'I went to University and studied law alongside my accounting degree. This was before I had a kid. Now, I can't even fathom doing that. Then, Erin and I started Grace House and it was clear she was better at the emotional stuff than me. I can handle finances, stakeholder meetings, contracts, going to court, negotiating prenuptials. Just don't ask me to talk to someone about their emotions.'

'And you?' she throws the question back at me. 'Clearly, you've just started as a barista.'

I look down at the scar on my palm and laugh. 'Yeah, that was my first shift. My first job really.'

'Did Laurie recognise the famous last name?'

'If she did, she said nothing,' I say. 'My Dad cut me off when I told him I was studying a bachelor of music composition instead of the law and political science degree he thought he was bankrolling. I had a couple of thousand stashed in a personal account, but I've spent most of it just trying to keep a roof over my head since January.'

'So you've been in the hostel for four months?'

I shrug. 'It's not so bad. You meet a lot of people.'

Ana's phone buzzes, and she turns, picking it up. I see the name JON WILLOUGHBY flash up on the screen. Wonder who that is.

'You can get that,' I say when Ana doesn't pick up.

She shakes her head. 'Not urgent, I'll call him back at the office.' The phone stops ringing, and Ana downs the rest of her coffee.

'Right,' she says, all business. 'Can I interest you in a ride back to Chapel Street?'

My head swims at the idea of finding my way through the suburbs in peak hour, so I happily take her up on her offer. We arrive at Grace House just before nine.

'Thanks for last night,' I say as we step out of her Mercedes. Instantly, I regret phrasing it that way. How cringe.

'It's fine. Are you working this morning?'

I nod. 'Yeah. Start at ten.'

'I might see you soon, then.' Her words are casual enough, but her tone sounds flirty. Feels flirty. There's a part of me that can't believe last night happened; that Ana picked me up off the street like a stray, housed and fed me.

'I'd like that,' I say. 'Besides, I'm pretty sure I owe you a coffee.'

CHAPTER FIVE

I watch as Jordan rounds the corner towards Laurie's. Once he's out of sight, I pull out my phone and call Jon. The line rings three times before he answers with a groggy, 'hello?'

I glance at my watch. It's almost nine in the morning. Clearly, it's been a big night.

'Jon, it's Ana.'

'Ana?' he repeats, as if he's waiting for his brain to catch up. Like I'm not the mother of his child. Like he's not spent the last week trying to contact me. 'Oh, oh shit, Ana. Hey. Guess you got my message.'

'Messages,' I correct. I didn't want to call him angry, but it's hard not to get agitated at his tone. I haven't heard his voice since one explosive phone call almost five years ago and hearing him now is like a throwback. 'And you know, you really have some nerve—'

'Listen, if you don't want me to see her, I won't,' he bites back immediately. He was always quick to anger.

It was always the least unattractive thing about him. That and all the cheating.

'I didn't say that.' I gotta keep my cool. Jon will only meet my energy if I get upset. 'She deserves to know her father, and if you're willing to make an effort—'

'I am,' he cuts me off. 'I just want to meet her.'

You could have met her the day she was born I want to say, but I don't. 'Royalla Park, nine-thirty tomorrow morning.'

'I'm working nights,' he replies. There's always something with him. Some excuse. Something I have to change to accommodate for him. So what if he's working nights? I work nine hours a day, and then some and still have time for my daughter. 'I'm AV for a show in Carlton. Don't normally get off until two or three in the morning.'

'Twelve-thirty then,' I say. 'There's a cafe in the park. I'll book a table.'

'Thanks,' Jon says. There's a pause on the other end, and then he says, 'so you've done pretty well for yourself, haven't you?'

I pinch the bridge of my nose with my thumb and forefinger. We are not having this conversation right now. 'Goodbye Jon. See you tomorrow.'

'Hold on!' Jon says just as I'm about to hang up. 'I wanna bring Poppy a present. What does she like?'

'She's four years old, Jon.'

'I don't meet many four-year-olds in my line of work, *Ana*,' he replies, adding a sarcastic tone to my name. 'What about a Barbie? Do they still make Barbies?'

When I found out Poppy was a girl, I decided to avoid the wave of pink that was inevitably coming my way. Not that I have anything against pink. It's a lovely colour. I just had no desire to paint a child's room a colour associated with their gender, nor have all my white business shirts-tinged pink from the washing.

Guess the colour my four-year-old is obsessed with? It's not that trendy oatmeal beige that seems to be all over Instagram these days. I believe the Greeks call that *hubris*.

'Clothes,' I say. 'She likes clothes. Pink ones. Do not get her a pair of sparkly pink gumboots. My sister's already getting her those for her birthday.'

'Something pink, then. Noted. Thanks.'

'See you on Saturday. Twelve-thirty.' Jon was always terribly late. Forgetful to the point of frustration. He confirms. It's the first conversation we've had in years, and neither of us tore each other's head off.

As soon as I hang up, reality sets in. I'm seeing the father of my child—a man I have not seen in four-and-a-half years—tomorrow. Twelve-thirty.

I take a deep breath, and then another and let it all sink in. Once I feel like I have a handle on myself, I push through the front door of Grace House. Immediately, Olivia catches my gaze from behind her computer. She pushes her copper hair behind her ear and stands up.

'Ana, Greg Pryor called again, and—'

'I'll call him back,' I say as I grab a mug and shove it under the spout of the coffee machine. 'Today. Promise. Need another coffee before I do it.'

The coffee machine runs, and I inhale the fresh scent of espresso. If I planned it now, Poppy and I could find somewhere to holiday over Christmas. We'd go somewhere warm. Rent a place with an ocean view, far, far away from Melbourne. Maybe Cairns.

But as I think about my mum, I dash any plans for a Christmas break. I'd hate to leave Mum on Christmas. She'd ask why we weren't there.

I take my coffee to my computer and open my emails. There's a message from Collette with the subject line thank you. Clicking on the email, a photo loads of her in front of her modest townhouse. She's surrounded by her friends, holding a bottle of champagne. Behind her, she's plastered a sold sticker on a 'for sale' sign.

A new life, she's written underneath the photo.

I zip up Poppy's coat as we set out to Royalla Park. It's a crisp, chilly day, and despite it being almost midday, the greyness hasn't left the city. Melbourne is beautiful year-round, but it holds a kind of magical quality in autumn. The fog that blankets the park only emphasises the vibrant gold of the oak trees. The air is cool and smells fresh and earthy. Poppy kicks through fallen leaves as we walk through the park, her old gumboots squelching along the muddy paths.

'Is Thomas going to be here?' she asks, tugging on my hand.

'No, I told you, we're meeting one of my friends from when I was younger,' I say. 'His name is Jon.'

'Jon,' Poppy repeats.

I refuse to call him her 'dad'. He's not her dad. Her biological father, yes, but 'dad' is someone who takes your kid to sport on Saturdays, who cooks dinner every second night, someone who teaches your kid how to tie their shoelaces. I take Poppy to her Auskick games, her tennis practice. I cook dinner every night and, well, we've only bought shoes with Velcro fastenings so far, but one day I'll tackle the shoe-tying. Or maybe Erin can teach her how to tie her shoes. Raising a kid takes a village, as they say.

Regret and worry curl like slippery fish in my gut. I don't even know what I'll do if he mentions the 'd' word in front of her.

We arrive at the playground. When I first bought Poppy here, she was only six months old. It's a no-risk, no-fall soft plastic hell-scape. There's absolutely zero risk of a grazed elbow. I don't know why. Grazed elbows are integral to childhood.

I really should take Poppy to a better park, but this one is close to the apartment, and it's got a cafe. Convenience and caffeine.

Tulip Café is a cute little shop; housed in a white weatherboard cottage with French windows. It's busy on a Saturday morning, but I've reserved a table in the courtyard. Poppy dashes towards the playground, unheeding my calls to stay close. She's met up with another girl who often comes to the playground, and I give her mother a small acknowledging wave. I don't know either of their names, but they've been coming to the playground for the last few weeks. Maybe I should make an effort. I resolve to ask Poppy.

Casting my gaze away from Poppy, I text Jon that we've arrived. A small slither of me expects him to text that he won't be able to make it. It wouldn't be surprising.

A young man comes to take my coffee order, and for a moment, I believe I see Jordan. This waiter is the same height—around six-foot, but he doesn't have that same crop of dirty blonde curls, the dimpled smile and smattering of freckles.

I order a latte and turn back to Poppy. She's climbed to the top of the slide and as she whooshes down it, her pink tutu flies up around her stockings and she laughs brilliantly. Yes, my daughter is wearing a tutu to the park. I have better things to do than argue with my daughter over why a tutu is not everyday attire. If my kid wants to wear a sparkly pink tutu twenty-four-seven, that's her prerogative.

'Hey, Ana.' I turn away from Poppy to find myself face-to-face with Jon. He's standing in front of me, shoulders slumped and holding a bright pink gift bag.

The first thing I think is how old he looks. His hair is grey, and he's cut it short. There are dark circles under his eyes; he almost looks unwell. He places a small gift bag on the table and, without being invited, sits in the chair beside me. The distinct smell of stale cigarettes wafts my way.

'So,' he says, looking over to the children playing on the playground. 'Which one is she? Oh, don't tell me, she's the one in the pink tutu, right?'

I seethe at his wording. Which one is she? Like she's a dog at a park.

'Told you, she loves pink.'

The waiter comes back with my latte, and I briefly wonder if I could ask him to make it Irish. Perhaps that's not the best look. It's not even one in the afternoon, but a naughty part of me wonders if he'd do it.

Jon orders a coffee for himself and relaxes into the flimsy chair. He's wearing an old grey shirt, stained, and torn at the hem, with a pair of faded black jeans and boots.

'So, why Poppy?' he asks. 'I thought you were set on

Briana.'

'She looked more like a Poppy when she came out,' I reply. Not that he would know.

The waiter brings Jon his coffee and I take a sip of my own, savouring the rich taste.

'Didn't expect you'd want to meet up with me,' Jon says as the waiter leaves.

'Didn't expect that you'd leave for work and not come back,' I reply before I think better of it. The corner of Jon's mouth twitches.

'That's fair.' He doesn't look me in the eye, but there's no malice in his tone. It surprises me. 'It was a shit move on my part.'

When I agreed to meet up with Jon, I knew we'd talk about the past together—how could we not? I knew it'd be hard, but I didn't think it would be this hard.

'Why did you do it?' I ask just as he says, 'I want to be a part of her life.'

For a second, I think I've heard him wrong. A part of her life? Now?

'You're joking.'

'Marianne, she's my child, too.'

'Don't,' I seethe. 'Don't call me that.'

He knows how much I hate being called by my full name. It's not my name. Not anymore. I know he's done it because he wants me to know he's pissed off with me. Classic manipulation. How quickly we fall into our old traps.

'She hasn't been your child for four years,' I continue. 'So don't even start with—'

'She's coming over,' Jon interrupts, his gaze focused on the playground.

I turn and see Poppy running through a mass of

golden leaves, her dark hair bouncing around her face. Her cheeks are rosy from the cold. She gives Jon a gentle but cautious smile as she approaches our table.

'Poppy, this is Jon. One of Mum's,' I pause, trying to think of the right word, 'friends.'

'Hey Poppy, it's nice to meet you.' He reaches out to shake Poppy's hand.

Poppy, who a moment ago, was a bucketful of charisma and confidence, sticks close to my side. 'Hi,' she says in a small voice.

Jon's handshake falls flat, so he grabs the pink gift bag and pushes it across the table. 'I got you a present. I hope you like it.'

Poppy grabs the bag without question. I sneak a look into the bag as Poppy opens it to check it's not too garish. Or inappropriate. Like a pink makeup set or a pair of those awful children's high heels.

Poppy pulls out the pink sparkly jumper and practically beams. It's horrendous.

'I love it!' she squeals.

'Wow.' I feign enthusiasm. 'This will match with almost everything in your wardrobe, Pops!'

Without missing a beat, Jon says, 'and, it'll go great with your tutu.'

'Mum, can I put it on right now?' she asks. The jumper is already halfway over her head by the time I say, 'yes.'

I shoot him a dirty look, and he has the guts to smile back. I almost burst out laughing at the cheekiness of it. It's surprising how we are still so similar. How it feels like no time's passed between our meetings. For good and bad. But then I look at Poppy and realise how long it has been, and how much hurt he's caused.

It's one thing to break up a relationship. It's not like we were married. But it's another thing entirely to leave your underemployed, pregnant partner to raise her daughter by herself.

The waiter returns with Poppy's hot chocolate, and I warn her not to get it on her new jumper before she dives in.

'So what year are you in at school, Poppy?' Jon asks.

'She doesn't go to school,' I interrupt. 'She's in preschool.'

'I'm going to school next year.' Poppy plucks a marshmallow out of the hot chocolate and eats it off her fingers. I remind myself to schedule a lesson on table manners when dining at a café. Maybe I could get her into one of those etiquette classes for young girls. The thought of etiquette classes is abhorrent to me, but knowing Poppy, she'd absolutely love it.

'So how long are you in Melbourne for?' I ask Jon. 'And where are you located these days, anyway?'

'Sydney,' he replies. 'And I fly back tomorrow morning with the band. I do all their audio visual. You might have heard of them—they're called the Noxious Species.'

It's a classic name drop. Noxious Species only won three ARIAs last year. 'I've heard of them.'

'She really looks like you,' Jon says, changing the subject. 'She's got your hair. Your eyes. I don't even think there's a slither of me in there. Does she know I'm—'

'Don't,' I warn. My heart's racing. Luckily, Poppy is too busy looking at a dog on the other side of the park to realise what Jon's just said.

He looks at me, a little confused. 'You haven't—'

'No. And it hasn't been asked about,' I say vaguely. 'So, drop it.'

That must let the wind out of his sails because he looks a little hurt. But honestly, she hasn't asked about him. She doesn't know other families well enough to know that most of the time there are two parents, and usually they're a mum and a dad. One day, that will change. Not sure what I'll say then.

'Right. I meant what I said before.' He looks at her before adding, 'I mean, I've paid support since she was born. Every year, I submit my accurate income statements and I pay on time. I'm not out here trying to cheat the system.'

Cheat the system. The phrase is like a trigger. Another popular Google search term other than 'help' and 'divorce' is 'avoid' combined with 'child support'. There are shitloads of blogs out there detailing the ways men can shirk their responsibility in ethically dubious ways—all from donating to charity to accepting more 'cash-in-hand' jobs to lower taxable income.

'You didn't even show up to court.' For two years, he paid the lowest amount of child support possible. I'd been a single mum trying to see my start-up through the first two years and caring for a newborn. Now I look back and I don't know how I managed. 'You didn't show up for any of it. My sister did. And Raf did.'

'Who's Raf?' Jon asked. 'Are you seeing someone?'

That's just the icing on the cake. I reach out to take Poppy's hand. 'Come on, Pops. We better head off.'

'Wait, Ana,' Jon says. 'Don't leave it like this. I just want to be in her life.'

I grab my handbag, not heeding Jon's complaints. 'Too bloody late.'

CHAPTER SIX

Grace House is the kind of place you'd walk past every day without noticing. Painted grey with subtle signage and blackout blinds always drawn, it looks like a funeral parlour. I suppose the people who come to Grace House need their privacy, but it makes me wonder why Ana would choose to run her business on Chapel Street. The rent must be astronomical.

As I open the door, I step into a large foyer. A woman sits on one of the two brown couches, thumbing through a magazine. She gives me a tight but polite smile as I close the door behind me. The air faintly smells of sandalwood, earthy and calming, and I notice a candle burning by a tea and coffee station. Soft instrumental music plays over the speaker system.

On the other side of the room, a woman with long copper hair looks up from her computer.

'Hello,' she says. 'Do you have an appointment?'

I cross the floor, feeling slightly uneasy as I do it. Maybe this was a bad idea. 'Ana told me to come in and ask for Erin.'

Recognition sparks in her green eyes, and she smiles. 'You're the barista?'

I nod. 'Jordan.'

'I'm Olivia,' she says and sits back down at her computer. 'Erin is just finishing up with another client, but she has most of the morning free. Take a seat and I'll see if she can fit you in.'

'Is Ana around at all?' I ask before I can stop myself. Don't know why I'm asking for her. It's not like we know each other that well. But it would be nice to see her.

'She's out with a client,' Olivia replies. Well, there's that hope dashed.

I take a seat across from the woman reading the magazine, and then my curiosity gets the better of me so I get up to investigate the coffee station. Free snacks don't come around often, so I make myself a coffee and take a Tim Tam. I pull out my phone and scroll on social media until the front door opens again, and a chime rings through the foyer.

Ana steps through the door. She's dressed in a black suit with a floral shirt, sleeves rolled up to her forearms. There's a large rose-gold watch on her right wrist. Her hair is loose, flowing around her shoulders.

'Hey you,' she says as she slides her sunglasses up. 'I'm glad you're here.'

'Me too,' I lie. Everything suddenly feels weird. My body thrums. The room, the people in it; it all seems far away. There's only Ana, standing before me, a half-smile on her mulberry lips. Maybe it was a mistake coming here. 'I'm just waiting for Erin.'

'Ah,' she says, as if it's a full sentence. 'Well, I'm glad you took up my offer.' Then, before I respond, she turns to the woman reading the magazine and invites her into her office.

Ana hands a coffee to Olivia as she passes her desk and continues down the hall. I finish my Tim Tam, and wait a little longer until Erin steps into the foyer. There's no mistaking Ana and Erin are sisters. They have the same long dark hair, but where Ana's features are angular and sharp, Erin has a rounder face and jawline. She's also curvier than Ana; and she's dressed more conservatively: a black knee-length skirt and blue button down. A stark difference to Ana's flashy and floral suit.

'Come on through, Jordan.' Her tone is quieter. Gentler. She guides me down the hallway. Photographs line the wall: cut-outs of newspapers immortalised. There's a photo of Ana and Erin and an older woman posing for a photo with the last prime minister.

'Ana's briefed me on your situation. Uni is such a stressful time,' she says.

I'm still lingering by the wall of photograph. Erin turns back. 'One of my favourites,' she says fondly as she comes to stand beside me. 'That's our mum, Grace, in the middle there.'

'She's the "Grace" in Grace House, then?'

'We built this place for her. For people who fall through the cracks.' She smiles, gazing at the photo. 'Mum didn't really know who she met that day. We thought it was because she didn't keep up on current affairs, but we found out a bit later she was in the early stages of dementia.'

'I'm sorry.'

Erin's mouth tightens into a long, thin line as she looks at the photo. 'There's not much we can do. She's well looked after at the home, and close by.' She steps away to open the door to her office. 'Shall we?'

Sunshine illuminates Erin's small office. A large monstera vine curls around a Victorian double-barred window. With a sigh, Erin sits down at her desk and motions for me to take a seat in one of the plush armchairs opposite her. I run my hands down the front of my pants. The nerves I felt earlier are back.

'Ana didn't really tell me what this meeting was about,' I begin. Honestly, I assume Ana's told Erin everything. The homelessness, the estranged family, the couch-crashing. 'Only that you could help me.'

Erin takes a long sip of her coffee as her other hand types a password into her laptop. Then, she places her coffee cup on a coaster and leans across the table. Her gaze is serious and overwhelming. I fight the urge to look away.

'Tell me about yourself.'

It sounds like more of an order than a question. 'What do you need to know?'

Erin looks back at her computer and I'm glad not to have her focus anymore. 'Why don't we start off with your income. How many shifts do you get at the cafe during a normal week?'

'Two. Three in a good week. But I also study full-time.'

It's hard to get comfortable in the chair, and I wiggle back and forth. There must be people who need Erin's time more. Not some kid cut off from the Bank of Mum and Dad, trying to make it as a musician.

Erin types my response into the computer. 'You apply for youth payment?'

I suck in a breath. 'Well, I did, but the people at the agency said I wouldn't qualify because my family earned too much. Even though I don't get a cent.' As soon as they'd clocked my last name, they'd scoffed. A Templeton needing support payments? What a joke.

Erin doesn't laugh. She doesn't even crack a smile. She types it all into her computer and then slides a clipboard across the table.

'When we take on new clients at Grace House, we sit down and determine their priorities,' she says. 'What they need right now to get them back on their feet, and then, what they need to live in a general level of comfort for five years—that's how long we estimate it takes someone to re-establish their lives. We're going to use your answers to create your success list.'

A success list. I've never thought about writing my goals before; giving them a rough timeline. When I graduated from high school, I only cared about getting to university to study music. Once I was there, I wanted to see how long I could study while Dad's money still flowed. Everything was day-by-day, week-by-week.

I look down at the paper, trying to think of my five-year goals and my mind wanders. I wonder what Erin's five-year goals are. Maybe if I asked her, it'd be easier to come up with my own.

'I don't really know,' I admit at last.

'Think about things that give you a sense of security. A job. A home.'

'I'm living in a hostel,' I reply. 'I assume Ana told you that.'

Wordlessly, Erin hands me a pen. I write housing security on my success list. Graduate university is second.

'Savings,' I say without being prompted. 'I don't really have any savings. You know, for rainy days.'

'So, savings of around five thousand dollars? You'd be able to go to university, meet your academic requirements and work a shift or two at Laurie's without worrying if you could pay for something if it went wrong.'

Five thousand dollars sounds good. It's not enough to afford to go on holiday, but it's a start of a financial cushion. I write the goal on the paper.

'And what do you want to be when you finish university?' she prompts. 'You know, once all this,' she waves her hand, 'is over?'

'I want to make music for films. TV shows. Compose film scores.' As I say it, I realise it's the first time I've ever told anyone about my dream job. I'd always worried someone would laugh or tell me it's unrealistic. Erin doesn't. She just types my answers into the computer.

Suddenly, her fingers pause over the keyboard, and she turns to me, an idea clearly in her head. 'Have you thought about performing?'

'What, like busking?' I ask.

Erin turns back to her computer, a sly smile on her face. 'Not exactly.'

My hand hasn't healed enough to pick up the piano again, so I switch to the guitar. It's easy enough. When I was younger, I'd fall into favour with instruments and just as quickly grow bored. Pianos, harps, lutes, saxophone, and, for a little while, a banjo. I'm convinced my habit kept a small family music shop in business, and my mother arranged lessons three times a week.

I stuck with six instruments long enough to play them confidently; piano and guitar are my strongest, followed by the violin and cello, and finally saxophone and clarinet.

Dad's disapproval was as stereotypical as it was hurtful. I was his only son; and he was an ex-rugby player. He had me in junior rugby as soon as I could run and hold a ball. When I didn't show a natural talent or enthusiasm, he'd encouraged me into academics. Debating. Mock United Nations programs. Mock courtrooms. Anything that would put me on a respectable and influential path as a politician or lawyer.

Much to his silent disapproval, my sister Megan and I were in the school choir, and we'd put on plays and recitals and sing carols at the local hall during Christmas. Megan moved out when I was fifteen, but by then we'd stopped the cheesy recitals and plays. I was much more interested in girls, and girls were much more interested in me if I had my guitar.

Who was Dad kidding? I was never becoming a politician.

I disembark the tram stop, slinging my guitar over my shoulder.

Lavender Gardens in Toorak is a beautiful facility. Like its namesake, the gardens are littered with various varieties of lavender and the air is heavy with their perfume. A nurse greets me at the gate and leads me to a spacious sunroom. A few of the residents play cards or knit, their eyes drifting up from their work as I step into the room. Football plays on a large wall-mounted TV. Demons versus Carlton. Dees are up by three goals.

'Set up where you'd like,' the nurse says. 'I'll get you

some water.'

I grab a chair from a card table and find a spot by the large bay windows. Tuning my guitar gets a few of the residents' attention, and a couple more wander in with the help of another nurse.

'You gonna play for us?' an old man calls from across the room.

'That's the plan,' I reply. 'Any requests?'

'*A Little Less Conversation*,' calls a young woman from the other side of the room. I immediately recognise the voice. Looking up, I see Ana perched on the arm of a recliner. Beside her, an old woman with dark grey hair sits with her legs covered with a garishly coloured crochet rug. I recognise her from the photograph. That's Grace.

A small child is working on a puzzle on the floor beside Ana. That must be her daughter.

I turn my focus back to the music. *A Little Less Conversation* is easy to play; I love its repetitive chords in A Major and once I'm into it, I'm really into it. More residents shuffle into the sunroom, lured in by the familiar tune. As the song ends, I launch into a rendition of *Bad Moon Rising*. While the residents may not know it, it's upbeat and fun, and to my surprise, a few of them get up to dance. The nurses begin to clap and Ana laughs, joining in.

I switch tactics, belting out a version of ABBA's *Dancing Queen*. It's not my best performance but everyone's dancing or singing along, drowning out my voice when it breaks on the high notes.

By the time I finish *Dancing Queen*, there's a real risk of wearing out my elderly audience, so I slip into a song by Frankie Valli and the 4 Seasons to mellow out the crowd. I risk a glance at Ana. Her braided hair is slung over her shoulder and she's wearing a pair of jeans and a black t-shirt. She meets my gaze. We smile at one another.

'Pretty good set,' she says afterward, approaching me as I make a coffee in the staff room. 'I thought *Wonderwall* was a bit overdone, though.'

I scoff. 'It's a classic for a reason. And it serves me well.'

'I bet it does.' She leans against the kitchen cabinet and plucks a strawberry left over from the residents' morning tea platter.

'What's that supposed to mean?'

Ana bites down on the strawberry. Her lips encircle the fruit, and I can't look anywhere else. Heat rises to my cheeks. God help me.

'I'm just saying,' she replies once she's swallowed. 'It's a douche anthem.'

'And I'm a douche?'

She scoffs. 'Please. You've never played *Wonderwall* to get laid?'

I open my mouth to reply, but then I remember evenings camping near Cape Reinga come back to me during Schoolies; nights I barely remember except for the taste of tequila, the feel of another body against mine, and the gentle chords of *Wonderwall*, which I may have played more than requested.

'Okay,' I admit. 'Perhaps there was a youthful dalliance.'

She snorts. 'You're twenty-two. Your life is a youthful dalliance.'

Ana picks up my coffee and takes a long sip. I give her a dirty look but grab another mug. 'Suppose I owed you a coffee.'

'Did Erin set this up for you?' she asks.

I nod. The kettle whistles as it boils. 'She said they'd pay me thirty bucks, but I'm not gonna accept the money. She also got me a job tutoring piano.'

'How many instruments can you play?' she asks incredulously.

The kettle clicks off its boil and I pour myself another coffee. 'A few.'

Ana's brow rises. 'Modest.'

'Was that your Mum and daughter out there?' I ask thought I have no reason to. Ana's personal life isn't something she has to share with me.

'Yes,' she replies. 'Poppy and I come here every few weeks. Erin swings by too. Oh! That reminds me.' She turns back to where her mother and Poppy are finishing a puzzle. 'Pops! Come here!'

Poppy looks up and scrambles to her feet. She looks a lot like Ana: dark hair and fair skin, and big brown eyes. She's as flamboyant a dresser as Ana is; sporting sequin rainbow shorts, a pink top and a pink cat-ear headband.

'Poppy, this is Jordan,' she says. 'Ask him if he'll play the song.'

I glance to Ana, eyebrow raised, before leaning down to talk to Poppy. 'Do you have a request?'

Shyness overcomes her. She hides behind her mother's leg as she says, 'Um, yes.'

'Ask him nicely,' Ana coaxes.

'I was wondering,' Poppy begins slowly. 'If you would... maybe play the Elsa song for me. From *Frozen*.'

'The Elsa song?' I echo. 'Oh, you mean *Let It Go*?'

'That's the one,' Ana confirms, hauling Poppy up onto her hip. 'We love *Frozen* in this house. We're a bit obsessed.'

'Do you think you could play it?' Poppy asks, feeling

braver.

'I'd have to look it up if that's okay,' I reply. 'I've never played it before, so I would probably have to learn it.'

'Well, we're here all the time,' Ana says as she runs a hand over Poppy's head.

A crowd of people swarm around a noticeboard in front of the lecture hall. I'm too far away to see what's written, but Marco emerges from the crowd and catches my eye.

'The composition prize is open again,' he says when he gets to me. 'Submissions close end of the month.'

The South Melbourne School of Arts Composition Prize is one of the most prestigious undergraduate competitions. Not only does the winner receive a cash prize, but several finalists land recording contracts, audition invitations for orchestras and musical theatre. The Composition Prize is one reason the South Melbourne School of Arts is so competitive; it's the best kick-start to a career in music, and every single undergraduate wants to win it.

'Are you entering again?' I ask Marco. Last year, he'd ranked third overall. As a first year, it was unheard of, but Marco's guitar skills are incredible and he's a brilliant songwriter. He scored a recording contract out of it and has spent most of the summer in a recording studio.

In contrast, I'd spent my summer mulling over ways to tell Dad I'd switched my degree; and getting drunk to avoid telling Dad I'd switched my degree.

'I think I'll give it a miss this year,' Marco says as we

take a seat in the lecture hall. 'But you should enter.'

I shrug. 'Depends if I can think of something to write. Creativity has been a bit lacking these days.'

'Something will come,' he says, even as he taps out a tune on the table. By the time the tutor enters the room, he's scribbling notes on an app on his tablet. By the end of the class, he has half a song written and I can tell he's itching to write more. It comes so easily to him.

It used to be like that for me. I don't remember the last time I wrote music.

Marco stops me outside the lecture hall. 'Feel like getting a drink?'

As much as I'd like to hang out with Marco, I don't have the money. 'Can't. Got a shift at the cafe.' It's a lie. I'd planned on working on an assignment at the library before heading back to the hostel.

'Why does a Templeton need to work at a cafe?' Marco scoffs.

'Dad doesn't bankroll me anymore,' I tell him, but I know he doesn't believe it. Marco's on a scholarship; a talented kid from the Northern Territory. Last year, we'd lived comfortably on the allowance Dad gave me, thinking I was studying law and politics. He'd been staunchly against telling him; against me doing this on my own. I can't blame him. We'd had money for booze, tattoos, drugs. Whatever we wanted.

'Shame. Come around on Friday, though. Bunch of us going into the studio. Be nice to see you.'

I nod. Marco's crew are all creative types: guitarists, songwriters, stoners. Maybe hanging with them will inspire a bit of creativity. 'I'll check my roster and let you know.'

He scoffs like my job is a joke to him.

'Jordan!' The lecturer calls me from inside the hall. We both turn out heads. 'Can I see you for a moment?'

'See you, Templeton,' Marco says, throws his bag over his shoulder and walks off.

The lecturer of Song Writing Fundamentals, Martin Delgado, pins me with a hard stare as I sit down in front of him. He's a short man who wears thin-framed glasses and ornately knitted jumpers. He thumbs through a folder of assignments. My stomach clenches nervously as he pulls mine out and sets it down on the table between us.

The word PASS is written in big block letters on the front of my paper.

Shit.

'I wanted to talk to you about your recent assignment.' He flicks through the pages. 'I'll be frank, I have concerns that this isn't your own work.'

Not my own work? Had I missed a citation somewhere? Had I quoted too much without referencing?

'I don't understand. The online portal didn't flag plagiarising. If I did, it wasn't intention—'

Martin raises his hand to silence me. 'I'm talking about essay writing services. I know students like you, Jordan. Students who come from backgrounds like yours, who have the money to invest in these kinds of services when they don't feel like putting in the effort themselves.'

Laughter bubbles out of me before I can stop it. Martin frowns.

'This is serious, Jordan.'

I clear my throat. 'My dad cut me off when he found out I was studying music. I'm even working with a temp agency to get a few odd jobs. Trust me, I'm broke. Whatever is in that essay, I wrote myself.'

Martin's face softens slightly and his eyes dart to the paper. 'I see,' he says after a long moment.

'I can give you the name of the agency if you'd like,' I continue. 'Despite the last name, I barely have enough money to afford three meals a day, let alone pay someone to write my essay.'

Martin lets out a long-suffering sigh. 'Well, it was quite a good essay.'

That's something at least.

Martin continues, 'Let me reassess it tonight. Last year, we had a case of essay fraud, and the writing was familiar for me, but I believe you. I'm sorry your family are not supporting your passions. I understand that can be difficult.'

'Nothing about this situation has been easy,' I admit.

'Sometimes when we're faced with hardship, we do our best work,' Martin says. 'And occasionally, it can zap all creative spirit from us. Tell me if either of those feel familiar.'

'If I can't play, I don't know why I'm here.' The words surprise me.

Martin slips the assignment back into his folder and takes off his glasses. 'Creativity inspires creativity; playing a little even when you don't want to, even if you're just running through what you already know, it can get those juices flowing.'

Martin's phone chimes, and he pulls it out of his pant pocket. 'Sorry, I have to go. My office hours are nine to eleven thirty on Mondays and Fridays. Feel free to come through any time.' He taps the top of the folder of assignments. 'Glad we sorted this out.'

I can't believe I've just had this conversation. 'Yeah, me too.'

CHAPTER SEVEN

I wake to the sound of the coffee machine running—in the apartment I live in alone with my daughter. It's barely six in the morning but I shoot out of bed and dash down the hallway. I find Poppy on her tiptoes near the coffee machine. Water gushes out from a coffee head, spilling down the side of the cupboard. Resolving myself to express curiosity and not anger, I approach her, my brain wild with worry. Has she consumed the nasty second-hand coffee water already? Do they make child locks for espresso machines? I'll investigate.

'What are you doing there?' I ask as I step into the kitchen. It's like approaching a wild animal. One wrong move and she could burst into tears.

'Making a coffee,' she says, like it's the simplest thing in the world. 'For you.'

Bless this child.

'Why don't I show you how to make one?' I nudge her to the side with my hip and immediately turn off the water. She's tall enough to reach things on the counter now, even if she's standing on her tiptoes. When did that happen?

I take the old coffee out of the head and throw it in the organic recycling bucket, wash the filter, and grind fresh beans.

'Now we tamp the coffee beans down,' I say, leveling the beans in the coffee head and flattening them. 'And we're all ready to go.'

'Can I have one?' she asks.

'Not until you're older.' I grab the Milo from the cupboard instead. 'Coffee is for adults. Like wine.'

She looks at me with an air of disbelief, one eyebrow slightly cocked, wariness reflected in her brown eyes. I take a sip of fresh coffee and stare down at the challenge.

'Fine,' she huffs out.

'You make breakfast, I'll make the milo.'

Poppy's been helping in the kitchen since she was eighteen months old. It all started when I walked into her early learning service to see her and a handful of other toddlers wiping down a table following afternoon tea. Never thought to let her do that, but apparently kids love to imitate, and they love helping. The next night, I gave my almost two-year-old a rag and watched as she wiped down our dining table after a messy pasta dinner. Never looked back.

My phone rings from the bedroom. It's barely six-thirty, so I let it ring off. After working nine hours a day—sometimes more—can spare an hour to eat breakfast with my daughter.

After dropping Poppy off at preschool, I park the car and walk down to *Laurie's* for a coffee. The morning is warm but overcast, and a spittle of rain hits my face as I push open the door of the cafe. Inside, it smells of vanilla and cinnamon, freshly cooked muffins. Cookies. And coffee.

'Hey you,' Laurie smiles, her hands busy at the coffee machine. She's pinned back her hair today, revealing bright blue hair underneath the layer of blonde. 'Jordan should be in any minute if you're waiting to see him.'

'We caught up the other day,' I say, sliding my reusable cup and ten dollars towards the till. 'Can I get two flat whites when you're ready?'

'Sure, anything else?'

A white-chocolate raspberry muffin seduces me from behind the glass cabinet, but I resist its wiles. 'Nope, that's it.'

'You've been busy?' I ask while she works.

She nods and huffs out a little laugh. 'I'm thinking about hiring again.'

At her words, a bolt of fear hits me. But then I realise she's talking about hiring *another* staff member, not necessarily replacing the one she's got, and I'm forced to face my sudden adverse reaction. And how strongly I'd felt about something happening to Jordan.

She slides the two cups across the bench. Suddenly, I'm keen to leave. I don't want to see Jordan. Not with how I'm feeling. Off-kilter. Overwhelmed.

It's not a shock to care for someone; to hope they don't lose their job.

But the thought that had run through my head immediately after Laurie spoke wasn't about his job, or his livelihood, but that there wouldn't be a reason for him to be around.

I'd never see him again.

'Thanks for the coffee,' I say to Laurie. 'Good luck with the hiring.'

'If you know anyone at Grace House, send them my way,' she says.

I promise to and go to leave. With my shoulder, I push open the door. It opens easily, almost effortlessly, but as I look up, I realise my mistake. Jordan does too. As our eyes meet, we both know it's too late.

His body slams against mine, a wall of muscle, and the coffee spills between us. Heat seeps through my blouse, my bra. Immediately, I regret wearing white.

'I'm so sorry,' Jordan says, his hands attempting to steady the leaking cups. Coffee runs down my front and spills onto the tiled floor. 'Ana, I'm so *sorry*. God, I didn't even see you.'

'It's fine,' I grit out and then berate myself for my tone. Getting angry will only make him more upset. 'It was an accident.'

I look down to survey the damage. My stained white shirt sticks to my skin like plaster, and while there are no noticeable stains on my black business pants, they're soaked and grow cold as the coffee cools.

'Shit, my handbag,' I mutter as I notice splash marks on the red leather. Erin bought this for my last birthday, knowing I'd never buy a designer handbag myself. I quickly grab a tissue and wipe it down, but the marks don't budge. Shit.

'I'll pay for it,' Jordan says immediately. He must see the brand name, must know how expensive it is. 'I'm so sorry.'

'Here you two.' Laurie holds out a packet of baby wipes. Her eyes glimmer with amusement. 'Why do you always cause some kind of predicament?'

'I couldn't see her through the tinted windows,' Jordan says as he wipes himself over.

'It's fine, really. It was a mistake.' After Jordan's first

accident and now this, I worry Laurie may actually consider replacing him.

Laurie huffs out a little laugh. 'Let me make you another coffee, Ana.'

I shake my head. The coffees cooled on my suit and the fabric sticks to me, itching uncomfortably. 'Leave it, I'd better go home and change.' I turn to Jordan and force a smile. 'Keep out of trouble for the rest of your shift, won't you?'

'I can't believe I just did that.' He looks genuinely miserable. 'I'm so sorry, Ana.'

I squeeze his shoulder in compassion and his hand covers mine. I feel the callouses of his fingers brush over the front of my hand. 'No use crying over spilt milk. It's fine, Jordan. Really.'

He gives me a commiserating look and lets out a long huff. With everything going on in his life, I suppose this is just another thing that's gone wrong. He walks out the back, pulling his stained grey shirt over his head. At least I didn't spill it on his uniform.

'I'll put it on your tab for next time,' Laurie says as she throws a few tea-towels over the mess.

'Don't be too hard on him,' I say. 'It was an accident.'

Laurie nods, her gaze casting towards her office door. 'He's a good guy. Maybe we need to sage him or something. Get rid of evil spirits that surround him.'

That makes me laugh. 'It's not a bad idea.'

Behind me, a man in a dark fitted suit walks into the cafe. The smell of lemongrass and musk follows him; his cologne delicate yet masculine.

'What's happened here?' he says in a deep voice, and to my surprise, he kneels down to help Laurie clean up the spill.

She's as surprised as I am. Her face flushes and she stutters out, 'Oh, Seojun, thank you. You don't have to do that.'

Leaving Laurie and Jordan, I decide to swing into the office to tell Erin about the ordeal before heading home. Luckily, we don't have clients waiting in the reception. Olivia bites her lip as I walk past, but doesn't make a comment.

Erin's in her office. I can hear her typing, the click-clack of the keys carrying down the hall. She must hear me walking because she calls out, 'Ana, Greg Pryor called *again* for you—you—what did you *do?*'

She takes in my appearance, her mouth slightly agape.

'Ran into Jordan during a coffee run,' I reply. 'Literally, ran into him.'

'I can see that.' She laughs a little.

'Don't laugh. He got it on my YSL.' I hold up the handbag she bought me, the coffee stains dotting the leather.

'Oh Jordan,' she drawls like she's on a sitcom.

'Laurie suggests we sage the bad luck out of him.'

Erin hums, 'I'll talk to him about creating a manifestation board in our next session.'

'Do that,' I say. 'I'm going to go home and get changed.' Erin goes to interrupt me, but I catch her. '*And* I'll call Greg back.'

It's not like I've been avoiding Greg Pryor, it's just that I only have so much time in the day, and I have no interest in giving him any of it. I'm purposefully ignoring him.

The drive home is a little quicker now that the peak-hour rush has lessened. I change my clothes, get back in my car and make it back to the office before lunch. At one, I meet a client, go over a plan to get her finances back in order after becoming the victim of identity theft, and then plan on tackling my inbox.

An unknown number flashes up on my screen just as I finish wolfing down a muesli bar. It's not unusual to get random calls. I give out this number to most people, and it's on all my business cards.

I answer, but before I can say hello, a woman sobs on the other end. Not good.

'Hello, this is Ana from Grace House,' I say in my most professional, compassionate tone. 'How can I help?'

The woman sniffs. 'It's Mel,' she croaks. 'Mel Wallace. I've just been served an eviction notice from Greg Pryor.'

Shit.

No wonder the bastard's been trying to contact me for weeks. Immediately, I regret not returning his calls for Mel's sake.

'I'm so sorry Mel, I had no idea he'd do this.' I try to keep my voice calm even as my heart races. 'What are the terms?'

'There are none. He's not renewing my lease, and it ends next month. He's given me thirty-days to leave.' Mel stifles a sob on the other end of the phone. 'What am I going to do? I can't move with a four-month-old baby.'

As angry as I am, I try to keep a level head. 'We're going to figure this out.'

'How?' Mel sobs.

I'm so angry with Greg. I know I need to call him, but I don't know how to get through the phone call without doing something I'll regret.

'I'm going to call Greg now,' I tell Mel. 'Just stay put.'

I hang up on Mel and thumb through my contacts until I find Greg's number. I take a deep breath and call Erin in.

'You're lucky. I was just about to leave,' she says as she walks into my office. She's wearing workout clothes, her long hair pulled into a messy bun, but one look at me and her face drops. 'What's happened?'

'Greg Pryor has evicted Mel and her baby.'

'Well fuck,' she says. 'Because of the new legislation?'

I nod. Five years ago, the government gave landlords tax breaks if they listed a percentage of their properties in line with government housing rates. The government waitlist is years long, and the incentives attempted to bridge a gap for people like Mel and her son, who couldn't feasibly live in shared accommodation.

Then a new government came in and scrapped the whole initiative because, why? Because fuck poor and vulnerable people, that's why. With the legislative incentives encouraging landlords to provide social housing now gone, there are fewer and fewer options available for people like Mel.

Now that incentive's scrapped, tenants are hinging their hopes on the goodwill of their landlords. Landlords like Greg Pryor.

'Can you sit?' I ask her. 'I don't know if I'm going to be the best version of myself on this phone call.'

Erin nods and takes a seat opposite me. With a shaking hand, I type in Greg's number. It rings twice before he picks up.

'Well, hello there.' The smugness is almost unbearable, and the thin thread of my patience snaps.

'What the *fuck*, Greg?'

Erin shoots me a stunned glare from across my desk and mouths my name in shock. I had warned her.

'It's not my fault, Ana,' Greg replies. 'I tried to call you at least a dozen times in the last few weeks to sort this out. I have all the phone logs, and not once did you call me back.' Greg doesn't mince his words. It's a polite threat that if I take him to the tribunal, he'll say he did his due diligence to inform me.

'So you evict my client?' I reply. 'Greg, she has a four-month-old baby.'

'So? Get someone to look after the kid while she moves her stuff. I gave her a legal eviction window.'

'You gave her a month. You gave her the *absolute minimum* you needed.'

'So?' he replies. 'Find her somewhere else to live. Isn't that what you people do?'

That's the only positive thing about this situation. Mel knows she has *us*. 'All this for an extra hundred bucks in your pocket? You're a selfish, greedy little man.'

He has the audacity to chuckle. 'Nice doing business with you, An—'

I hang up on him, livid. It's not fair. Mel has been a star tenant since she moved in almost twelve months ago, and then a piece of shit landlord like Greg, who values money over human decency, has the audacity to evict her. All in the name of chasing higher rental revenue. Nothing about this situation is fair.

The worst part about it is that I have no idea how I'm going to help Mel.

'That went well,' Erin quips. 'Nice, polite conversation.'

I roll my eyes, my rage now going unchecked. 'I hate him.' I run my hands over my face. Can this day get any worse? 'You can go. Don't make me be the reason you're late for your spin class. I gotta call Mel back.'

Erin nods and grabs her handbag. 'Good luck. You can pass Mel's case onto me if you'd like. I know we have our audit coming up.'

'Thanks, I'll consider it.' It might be best, considering my feelings for Greg Pryor. Erin leaves and I grab my phone, saving Mel's number before calling her back.

She picks up immediately. 'Do I have to move?'

'I think so, I'm sorry, Mel.'

'You can't do anything?' she demands. 'Take him to court?'

'The law's on his side, unfortunately. Let's meet next week and plan. We've got some time; we'll find you a new place.'

'We have *thirty days*,' she emphasises. 'Ana. I have a baby. He's enrolled in daycare around the corner. I'm going back to work in two months. If we can't find a place to live, what will we do?'

'We'll find a place,' I assure her.

I can hear the baby crying in the background. Mel flusters. 'We'll meet next week.' The baby cries louder. 'You better go. I'll text you my availability.'

I hang up and finally let myself slump against my office chair. What a day. I glance at the clock; it's just after five. Time to turn off the work brain and be a mum again. With a huff, I grab my soiled handbag, slip in my laptop into my handbag, and grab my car keys.

The next day, I spend hours calling my contacts in

real estate and social housing to find a place for Mel. I'm on the phone with a lady from the Department of Housing when Erin walks into my office and places a coffee on the table. I give her an appreciative smile, but she just shakes her head in disapproval once she realises I'm working Mel's case. I know she thinks I should give the case to her; that I'm too close to handle it properly, but I see so much of myself in Mel.

I see a single mum trying to raise a baby and have a career - not by choice but necessity. I see a woman who doesn't have the community I did; who doesn't have a sister who takes in their child every other Friday night.

I have to do everything I can to help Mel.

'I'm feeling like Mexican and then a movie,' Erin says as she walks into my office at a quarter-past-four. 'Has Poppy seen the latest Disney release?'

'Nope,' I reply as I finish typing an email. 'She's been begging to see it for two weeks now.'

'Excellent,' Erin replies. 'Raf wanted to go to the latest *Fast and Furious* film. I told him it wasn't appropriate for a four-year-old.'

'Poppy would have loved it,' I snicker. 'You're catching up with Raf?' It shouldn't bother me; Erin and Raf are good friends, and it is Erin's Friday with Poppy. But I feel a bit miffed I wasn't invited.

'Yeah. Just a casual movie thing.' She pauses. 'You got any plans?'

The whole point of Erin taking Poppy every second Friday was for me to have a social life. To go out. See people. Do things. But recently, it's been the only free-time I've had to workout and catch up on TV.

'No,' I respond. 'No plans.'

'Well, enjoy the night in,' she says.

Erin leaves soon after, and I focus on clearing out

my inbox before the week ends. It's later than I'd like it to be by the time I finally switch off my computer and grab my now sour-smelling handbag. I remind myself to put it in for dry cleaning.

It's dark outside, but the evening is crisp, and the sky is clear—the perfect autumn evening. A tram stops a few metres down the road, and a group of young women get off and head towards the nearest pub. One wears a sequined dress; the warm streetlight shimmering off her, scattering tiny rainbows on the ash vault.

Lingering by the door of Grace House, I watch as they fumble with their IDs in front of the bouncer. I used to be like that, used to wear tiny skirts on bitter days and drink so much I couldn't feel a thing. I'd stay out until sunrise with my friends; we'd go to basement gigs and weekend-long festivals. That's how I met Jon, a suave AV technician who played the bass in a band.

Our summer fling changed my life, but it barely impacted his.

I turn back to Grace House and lock the door.

'Hey!' someone calls down the road. Fisting the keys, so that one emerges between each finger, I steel myself and turn around.

'Ana!' Jordan calls, a half-a-block away from me.

I relax my grip on my keys and slip them back into the handbag. Jordan half-jogs towards me. He's in Laurie's uniform: light-washed jeans and a teal and pink striped t-shirt. With his curly locks and pink cheeks, he looks like he should in an old-timey quartet. 'You just getting off?'

His mouth twitches into a smile at my phrasing. Damn him. 'Just finished actually. You too?'

'Yeah, big day,' I reply. 'Frustrating day.'

He looks past me to glance at the line into the pub and says, 'Why don't we get a drink, then?'

My immediate response is to reject him. Say no. He's a client, and Erin's always reminding me about getting too close with clients. A social drink is definitely toeing the line.

But then Erin's words from this afternoon float back to me; *you got any plans?* And I remember the way she'd looked when I'd told her I didn't. Her tight smile. Her slightly worried gaze. Most of all, I recall the way I'd felt when she said she was going out. Sure, it might have just been for a movie; but she had plans, and I didn't.

'Sure,' I say to Jordan. 'One drink.'

He smiles like it's a challenge. 'One drink. I know just the place. Follow me.'

Jordan leads me across Chapel Street. It's busy so I stick close. Now and then, I get a waft of his cologne; woody and rich, and I'm surprised by how much I like it.

'So,' I say as the silence between us edges on the wrong side of comfortable. 'How was your shift?'

'Hmm?' he looks at me, clearly stuck in his own head. 'Oh yeah, it was good. Busy, but good. I just finished a tutoring session a few blocks away, actually.'

'Guitar?'

'Banjo,' he corrects with a laugh. 'Weird, I know, but the kid's good at it. And there's a shortage of banjo teachers around.'

I laugh. 'Who would have thought.'

Jordan slows down as we come to a hole-in-the-wall bar called *Walter's*. 'This is it.'

The bouncer asks for Jordan's ID but waves me through. I huff. Once, it was an insult to be carded.

Now it's a compliment. I know I don't look eighteen, but he could have carded me as a courtesy.

The bar is bigger on the inside; large Edison bulbs bathe the long bar in a warm light and soft rock plays over the speaker system. Deer antlers and US car number plates fill the walls. We pass the long bar, pass men playing pool, pass empty booths and a waitress who gives us a polite smile until we arrive at a large wood-log door. It looks like someone has ripped it off a Snowy River cabin.

As soon as I don't think *Walter's* can possibly get any bigger, Jordan opens the door to reveal an enormous room bathed in fluorescent lights. Noise floods out; loud rock music, people laughing and a steady *thump, thump, thump*.

'I thought we could work off the week,' he says as I step through the door.

'Really?' I reply as I take in the room. Cages line the far wall; a paper target in each. 'Axe throwing?'

'Yeah,' Jordan says, undeterred and obnoxiously positive. He walks over to the large Viking-themed bar and gets the attention of the bartender. 'Beer?' he shouts back at me.

I guess I agreed to *one* drink; I just didn't realise how many strings it'd came with. 'Sure. A pale ale, thanks.'

The bartender slides two steins across the bar— again, should have specified what size beer—and Jordan pays for a turn in the cages.

I've never thrown an axe before, so I listen to the instructions from the barkeep clearly: keep my feet behind the line, hold the axe with two hands and throw it over my head. Easy.

Once we've both agreed and signed waivers, he hands us a bucket of axes and directs us to cage eight.

'Ladies first?' Jordan suggests as he sips his beer. 'Or do you need a demonstration?'

'A demonstration would be nice,' I reply, setting my drink down on the bar table and sliding onto the stool.

Jordan grins and grabs an axe from the bucket. They're small, but as I grab my own and run my thumb-pad over the edge, I'm surprised at the sharpness.

In front of me, Jordan considers his position; he adjusts the placement of his feet, the way he grips the axe handle, and then relaxes the tension in his shoulders. The muscles in his back tense. With a small grunt, he throws the axe forward.

It hits the inner ring with a *thud*.

'Very impressive.' I clap. The computer updates his score.

'Thank you,' he says as he retrieves the axe and saunters back over to the bench. He grabs another from the bucket and flips it so the handle faces me. 'Your turn.'

I take a long sip of my beer before grasping the axe handle. I take it from him, and he grins. As I step up to the line, our shoulders brush and I lean into it, nudging him. He scoffs.

'Careful now,' he warns.

Stepping to the throw line, I go over the bartender's instructions. The axe feels heavier than it did before and for the first time, I worry I might not be good at this. That I might look like an idiot in front of Jordan.

'You can do it!' Jordan calls from behind me. 'Square your feet a little more!'

I glance down at my feet. He's right. I'm too angled. Squaring up, I raise the axe over my head, practising a few throws without letting go. Then, when I feel like I have the momentum, I fling the axe towards the target, aiming at the bullseye.

The blunt end of the axe hits the top of the target. It clatters as it hits the ground.

I missed.

Completely missed.

Damn.

'Bad luck,' Jordan says as I retrieve my axe. The computer shows a big fat zero against my name. 'Next time, think of someone who's wronged you.'

'Is that the secret?' I ask as I pick up my beer. I take a long drink and try not to think about the shitty throw. Try not to let it show how bothered I am about it. Being a sore loser isn't one of my most flattering personality traits.

Jordan throws again. His shirt rides up slowly, revealing a strip of his lower back. I'm so distracted by it, I don't even realise the axe has hit close to centre until Jordan whirls around, a glorious grin on his face.

The computer updates his score. He's well in the lead.

I grab an axe and step to the throw line. 'Show me how you do it.'

'Sure,' Jordan says as he comes behind me. I feel the heat of his body against my back, and not for the first time, I'm surprised at how tall he is. He looks down at me, his bright eyes roaming my body. Suddenly, my face feels hot.

'Square up; widen your stance; engage your core,' he directs.

I look down and adjust my footing again, spreading my legs and squaring my body. Jordan moves with me.

'Raise the axe.' His voice drops an octave. I've never heard him speak like this. So commanding. So authoritative.

As I raise the axe above my head, he steps away from me. The heat of his body's gone. I almost miss it.

'Eyes up,' he directs.

I focus on the target, but I can still see him in my peripheral. He's beside me, arms folded over his chest. Muscles ripple under Laurie's pinstripe shirt. 'Focus on the target.' There's a playfulness in his tone I can't ignore. He knows what he's doing.

I look back at the target, the axe raised over my head.

'Breathe out as you throw. Engage your core.'

Taking a deep breath in. I concentrate on the bullseye. On my exhale, I throw the axe forward. It spins in the air one, two, three times, before lodging just left of the bullseye.

'Whoo!' Jordan hollers, his voice carrying through the large auditorium. 'You did it!'

He raises his hand for a hi-five, and I slap it. I did it. I fucking did it. The computer updates my score as we go back to our drinks.

'So, who'd you think of?' Jordan asks. At my bewilderment, he motions to the target. 'The dude who wronged you. Who was it?'

'Oh,' I reply. 'Well, no one, really.'

He gives me a disbelieving look. 'That many, huh?'

I know what he's insinuating. 'It's a normal number of dudes. Don't worry.' Throwing it back to him, I say. 'Who are you picturing?'

He picks up an axe and considers it thoughtfully. 'My dad. He's a real pain in my ass.'

I already know Jordan and his father don't talk. 'Sorry to hear that. I can sympathise.'

Jordan's brows raise. 'Never had a good relationship with your dad?'

'He was abusive,' I say. 'Mainly to my Mum. They moved here from Czechoslovakia, well, when it was Czechoslovakia. She learnt English, got a job as a schoolteacher. Enjoyed her life. He didn't adjust so well. One night, he came home and hit me when he couldn't find Mum. We left the next day.'

'Jesus,' Jordan mutters. 'Where is he now?'

I shrug. 'Don't know. Erin thinks he might have gone back to Europe; she was only two when he left. We haven't heard from him since we were kids, and I don't think he contacted Mum again.'

I take a sip of my beer to ease the tightening of my throat. I haven't told that story in a long time; or thought about Dad.

'I'm sorry you went through that,' Jordan says.

I wave off his sympathies. The moods shifted and I don't like it. 'It's fine. It's your throw, right?'

After my coaching, I throw twice more and land both of them. But by some miracle, Jordan throws a bullseye and just scores a smidge more than me.

I finish my beer as Jordan comes back to the bench with his prize: a cheap stuffed bear.

'For you.' He pushes the bear across the table. I pick it up, feeling it's rough polyester fur.

He's won a bear for me. Like we're at a fair.

'I thought Poppy might like it,' he says.

'She'll love it,' I say, and I mean it. It might be

stupid looking, with its beady black eyes, but he won it. 'Thank you.'

Jordan gathers our empty steins. 'Well, that was a great 'one drink',' he says smugly.

'It was.' I give the bear one last look before slipping it into my stained handbag. 'That's why it can't happen again.'

CHAPTER EIGHT

It can't happen again.

It's been four days, but I can't stop thinking about those words. Or the way she'd looked at me when I'd ordered two steins of beer; or how she'd whooped after almost landing a bullseye.

You're a client. I want to keep things professional.

I push Ana out of my mind and focus on finding my way through the streets of Cranmore. A mix of modern townhouses and Victorian terraces line the narrow streets. Jacaranda trees blanket parked cars in purple petals, beams of sunlight filtering through the thick canopy.

I bring up Talia's email and read over it again. *19 Trail Street; look for the emerald door and the cow pot plant.*

There's a milk bar on the corner; advertising a $10 coffees and bacon and egg deal. The smell of fresh bacon wafts through the slightly ajar door.

Finally, I find 19 Trail Street: a Victorian terrace house with a garishly green door. A geranium grows out of a cow-shaped pot plant by the door, blooming crimson flowers.

After wiping down my sweaty hands on my shorts, I ring the doorbell and immediately hear footfalls inside. The door flies open and a woman—Talia—appears. She wears denim shorts, a crochet crop top and a thick fluffy cardigan. Dreadlocks fall around her shoulders; they're long and caramel at the end, occasionally adorned with golden cuffs and twists.

'Jordan?' she asks. When I confirm, she opens the fly screen door for me. 'Come on in.'

Talia waves me down a long, narrow hallway. My shoes echo on the floorboards and I briefly wondered if I should have taken them off.

'Rent is eight hundred a month,' she says over her shoulder. 'We halve all bills.'

We pass by the kitchen; it's a bland DIY-assembly kitchen not in keeping with the history of the home. 'I work Sundays through Friday at the hospital,' she says, pointing to her roster on the fridge. 'Usually night shift.'

At the end of the hallway, there's a large extension to the home. To my right, a bookcase is packed to the brim, and someone has perfectly positioned two chairs to catch the early morning sunlight. To my left, Talia opens a door and reveals a dark room.

'The current guy is moving out by the end of next week,' she says. 'You can move on Monday if you'd like.'

I step past her and peer into the bedroom. It smells stale, slightly of cigarettes and old coffee. Sunlight lines the edges of the shutters, desperate to burst in. Talia turns on the light and reveals a cheap bedframe and mattress pressed up against the wall. A desk with at least nine cans of energy drink—empty or not, I can't tell—is pushed up against the far wall. Small piles of clothes litter the room.

'So,' Talia says. 'You want it or not?'

I feel that anyone would be better than the house-mate she's currently got. 'You don't want to know about me?' I ask. For all she knows, I could be a murderer.

She raises one dark eyebrow. 'You a murderer?'

'No.'

'Can you pay your rent on time?'

'Yes.'

She shrugs. 'That's all I need. You want it or not?'

I look back at the dingy bedroom. Maybe once it's cleaned out and the shutters are open, it'll look better. Besides, it's close to university and work. Even if Talia turns out to be a shitty roommate, isn't that part of the experience? It's not like I'm in the position to be picky. 'Yeah. It looks good.'

'Great,' she replies, pulling her phone out of her pocket. 'I'll take down the ad. You can move in next weekend.'

My weekly meeting with Erin rolls around again and I'd be lying if I said I was looking forward to it. Since there's time to kill and I'm not keen on the idea of waiting in the lobby at Grace House, I decide to pop into *Laurie's* to take a photo of my roster. Laurie normally emails it to me anyway, but I figure I have the time.

As I step into the cafe, the bell by the door rings. A man stands in front of the coffee machine, and his gaze lazily moves from Laurie to me. I recognise him instantly as the guy who helped clean up the coffee I spilt over Ana.

He's handsome; tall with dark hair and a toned physique. A large floral tattoo winds up his sculpted left arm. He's dressed in a tight black tee and dark brown chinos. There's an access card attached to his belt, the kind issued by government and investment firms.

Laurie looks over the coffee machine, her face flushed red. I'm not sure if it's from access card man or the steam from the steam wand, but she looks flustered.

'You're not in today,' she says.

'I know,' I say as I step into the dining area. 'Thought I'd take a photo of my roster. Got some time to kill.'

Laurie nods and looks between me and access-card man. 'Jordan, this is Seojun.' She indicates to me with a nod. 'Seojun, this is Jordan, my newest hire.'

'About time you got some help,' Seojun says, not unkindly. Laurie slides the coffee across the bench and he takes it; sips on it, smiles. Everything he does is in one smooth motion and Laurie's gaze follows. Definitely wasn't the steam from the coffee machine causing that blush.

Seojun turns to me. 'Nice to meet you.'

'You too,' I fumble out.

Seojun leaves, the heels of his oxfords tapping on the tiles as he strides across the cafe floor. When the doors close behind him, I turn back to Laurie but she's disappeared.

I find her in the kitchen. She's busying herself by stacking the dishwasher, her back to me.

'He's cute,' I say as I lean on the kitchen doorway. 'And he likes you.'

She fumbles a cake tin and it falls to the floor. 'He doesn't.'

'Why don't you just ask him out?'

She scoffs as she closes the dishwasher. 'He's not interested in me, and even if he was, I don't date my regulars.'

I wonder if Ana counts as a regular. Reckon she does. 'Does that rule apply to me, too?'

She glares at me. 'Why? What have you done?'

'Nothing.' It's not a lie. Ana stopped it before it could become something.

'Don't mess with my regulars,' Laurie warns me again, but I can't take her seriously. Not with how she looked at him; how he'd looked at her as he'd taken a sip of coffee. It felt like I wasn't in the room. Laurie empties one of the coffee heads and lets out a little sigh. One might call it forlorn. 'You want a coffee before you leave?'

Not gonna turn down a free coffee.

When I enter Grace House, Olivia, the strawberry-blonde receptionist, peeks over the top of her computer screen.

'Erin's still with a client,' she says. 'You're welcome to take a seat.'

'Is Ana in?' I ask.

Olivia shakes her head. 'She's offsite for today, but I can let her know you asked for her.'

'No,' I say. 'No, don't worry about it.' I don't need Ana thinking I've come in asking for her.

It can't happen again.

I take a seat and sink right into the lounge cushions. Instead of the usual flute, this time, lo-fi plays over the speaker system; a mix of soft piano and bass. I flick through some of the adult colouring books, then a gossip magazine before pulling my phone from my pocket and scrolling through Instagram.

Marco's posted a string of photos of his friends hanging in a recording studio; lounging in the booth, scribbled out pages of lyrics, and one soulful photo of him singing into the microphone. I can't help but feel jealous. Marco's not the musician I want to be, but I'd do anything to feel like I was making real music.

I haven't written anything in months.

Maybe I should take up Marco's offer to hang with his friends. Network. Make connections. Be around other creative people.

'Jordan?' Olivia calls. 'Erin's ready to see you now.'

As I pass her, Olivia hands me a magazine. 'Can you give this to her? She's been with clients since lunch and I didn't want to interrupt her.'

Olivia hands me a copy of INFLUENCE magazine. My mum reads this religiously. A group of women grace the cover, all dressed in various shades of pastel. It takes me a minute to notice one of the women is Erin; and beside her is Ana. They look so different. They look glamourous. Formidable. Beside them, the subheading reads, *Australia's most influential women.*

'Looks good, doesn't she?' Olivia says, noticing my focus.

'They both do.' I clear my throat, embarrassed that I'd been so readable. 'I'll give it to her.'

Erin's wolfing down a sandwich when I knock on her ajar office door. She swallows and smiles, waving me in.

'Sorry, I'm absolutely wall-to-wall with clients and

meetings today,' she says as she puts away the rest of her lunch. 'How's things?'

'Good,' I say as I hand her the magazine. 'Olivia asked me to give this to you.'

Erin wipes her hands on a napkin and picks up the magazine. 'Oh!' she says as she thumbs through the pages. She clears her throat and begins to read, 'A lawyer, accountant, CEO, mother, and mentor, Ana and her sister, Erin.' She scoffs. 'Nice of them to mention me.'

She continues reading. 'The sisters opened Grace House in 2017. Grace House was named after their mother who experienced domestic violence while the sisters were growing up. Now, Grace House works to support at-risk people struggling with housing, financial stability, mental health issues, and all the other complex stuff life throws at us...' She clears her throat and closes the magazine, but keeps hold of it. She holds it and looks at it like it means something. Something more than just words on a page.

'Well,' she says after a moment, her voice wet with emotion. 'That's one for the hallway, isn't it?'

CHAPTER NINE

I finally make good on my promise to go to the hairdresser.

Poppy lets go of my hand and dashes ahead, bursting through the double doors of Raf's salon. She leaps into his arms and shrieks as he twirls her around. Raf deposits her into a salon chair as I walk through the door.

'Now, Miss Poppy,' he says, running his hands through her long brown hair. 'What can I do for you today, my girl?'

'Pink!' she replies instantly. Raf gives me an apprehensive look.

'Pink?' he repeats, his tone rising in mock outrage. 'Well, I love pink as much as the next person, but don't you think your sparkly pink jumper and pink tutu might clash with your pink hair?'

She laughs. Clearly not.

He throws a pink apron over her shoulders and pulls over his cart. 'Just a trim?' he asks me. 'It's gotten long.'

'A good few inches,' I reply. Frankly, I don't know the last time Poppy got a haircut. 'Best to give it a good chop.'

I sit in the chair beside Poppy and watch Raf work. No one would bring their child to Raf's salon for a haircut; not with the prices he charges these days. It was only four years ago we were living in a tiny apartment, barely making ends meet. Now, thanks to social media, he's styling celebrities and jetting off to work fashion weeks.

Briefly, I wonder who the more difficult client is: a four-year-old child or the celebrities and models he styles on the regular. As he attempts to make small talk with Poppy, I'm leaning towards the child.

'So, any boyfriends?' he asks as he leads Poppy over to the basin.

'She's barely in school,' I reply as I grab a magazine from the coffee table.

'I was asking you,' Raf quips back.

'Don't have time for a boyfriend,' I reply, flicking through the magazine until I find a free perfume sample stuck to the page. I pocket it before Raf notices. 'Do you have a girlfriend?'

Raf sticks his tongue out as he shampoos Poppy's hair. 'No one serious.'

I'm not surprised by his no-answer answer. Erin and I have known Raf for years, and I've never known him to have a serious girlfriend. Looking the way he does—tanned skin, curly brown hair, and dark eyes—I can't imagine he'd have any trouble finding someone interested in him. Maybe he just has a string of casual lovers; not interested in committing to any one person. I could see that for him.

'No boyfriend, and not interested,' I say. 'Too busy.'

Raf hums as if he's not convinced. He leads a dripping Poppy back to the salon chair and begins trimming her wet ends. I marvel at how long it's got. It really has been a long time since we had a trim. That's one point for bad mum bingo.

When Raf finishes blowing out Poppy's hair, he sighs dramatically at the curls scattered on the floor. 'Should have called the apprentice.'

I squat his shoulder as I grab a broom from the back of the salon. 'I'll do it. Let the girl have a single day off.'

I sweep Poppy's hair into a small pile, then make sure she's adequately entertained with colouring in before taking a seat in Raf's chair. He runs his hands through my hair and tuts.

'Long time since you've had a cut, too.'

'I've been busy.'

'Too busy for a boyfriend, too busy for a haircut.'. He pushes my hair over my shoulder to emphasise its length. 'Are we doing a colour today? There are a few strays up here. But the salt and pepper look would be lovely on you, darling.'

'Colour me up,' I say.

Raf looks down at my hair, studying it. 'Few layers? It's a bit thick.'

'Whatever you'd like.' I trust Raf knows what he's doing. Besides, it's only hair. It'll grow back.

'Right,' he says like he's settled on a plan. 'I'll go mix the colour.'

Once Raf steps away, I pull out my phone and check my emails. It's a Saturday and Mel's inspecting an apartment with a landlord still offering below-market rentals. If she likes it, it could be a good short-term option.

'I know someone.' Raf saunters back the room, colour pot in hand.

'You always know someone,' I reply. 'It never ends well.'

Whether they're the lawyer I dated two years ago, or the journalist who stood me up on our third date. No one Raf ever suggests is worth the hassle. Still, it doesn't deter him.

'Seriously, he owns a yacht,' Raf says as he applies the colour. 'And sure, maybe he's a little older than you, but maybe that's what we've been doing wrong! You just need someone who is a little older. A bit more established.'

He says it like he's been orchestrating a plan. 'I'm not interested in going out with anyone else you recommend. I'm sure you remember the model?'

'Now, how was I supposed to know Antonio was in a relationship?' he mutters as he studies my split ends. 'Two inches off?'

My phone buzzes in my handbag, and I glance at Rafael's reflection. He gives me a stern look that screams, can't you take a weekend off?

'I'll be quick, I promise,' I say before diving for my phone. He drops his brush in the colour pot dramatically.

'I needed to mix more colour anyway. There's a lot more to cover than I thought,' he huffs as he heads to the back room. 'Poppy, dear, do you want a juice?'

As soon as I pick up the phone, I regret it. Jon's name flashes up on the screen. He wants to know what Poppy and I are doing today, and if we'd want to go to the park again. Quickly, I type back the address of Raf's salon—where we'll be for the next hour, at least—and toss my phone back into my purse.

'So, Jon's back in town,' I say as Raf comes back.

Raf looks up from where he's mixing colour, scandal written over his face. 'You lie.'

'Nope. He said he wants to be a part of her life.'

Raf lets out a frustrated laugh and shakes his head. 'I can't believe him.' His eyes dart to Poppy who is, thankfully, still enthralled in colouring. 'What a D-I-C-K-F-A-C-E.'

I can't help but agree. 'Well, that D-I-C-K-F-A-C-E will be here in a minute. I've said he can take Poppy to the park down the road.'

'What?' Raf says. 'No wonder you're going grey.'

I snort. 'A-S-S-H-O-L-E.'

He kicks the bottom of my chair, and I stifle a laugh.

To my surprise, Jon actually comes through on his promise. He shows up wearing basketball shorts and a hoodie, freshly showered and shaved. Completely different from the Jon I met in the park a few weeks ago.

Raf does a good job of being civil. He's never met Jon, but he's heard enough about him to have formed a less-than-favourable opinion of him. Raf was my first roommate after Jon left, and we'd lived in the run-down apartment until Poppy was six months old. Few guys would be cool living with a baby, but Raf took it in his stride.

'Right, we'll see you at twelve?' Jon says as he takes Poppy's hand.

I look at Raf, and he nods, confirming we'll be done by then. 'Sounds good.'

'Thanks again, Ana.' He looks down at Poppy and smiles. 'Maybe we can get lunch later?' He's posed the question to Poppy and not me.

Before I can protest that we have lunch at home, and I have work to do this afternoon, Poppy says, 'Yeah!'

'Maccas?' Jon eggs her on. He wants to be fun, it's almost too much.

'Maybe we can talk about it at the park,' I say. 'It's supposed to rain this afternoon, so you better get going.'

Jon nods and leads Poppy out of the salon. As the door closes, I let out a long sigh and fall back into Raf's chair. 'You got any alcohol around here?'

Raf laughs. 'Sadly, no. It's also barely eleven o'clock. How about a coffee?'

'If that's all you have,' I mutter. Raf makes us both a coffee and hangs in the salon chair beside me while I marinate in my colour.

'I don't remember the last time I made a client a cuppa,' he chuckles as he sips his coffee. 'Or cut their hair.'

'Big shot hairstylist, too good for a cut and a colour now.'

'Big shot accountant, too good to do my taxes anymore,' Raf shoots back.

'Fuck you,' I laugh.

Didn't get the apartment, Mel texts me on Monday morning.

Shit.

The rental market is ridiculous.

For the last two hours, I've emailed, called, and followed up on rentals in my Mel's budget across the city. Mel and her son have just under twenty days to find another rental, but the market is in crisis. Two-bedroom apartments are almost Mel's entire weekly salary, and the kid will be in pre-school before she gets through the public housing list. Unless she wants to live in a share house in Dandenong, I've gotta come up with another solution and fast.

I take a sip of my mocha, savouring the warmth as I type out an email to Ian, a real estate friend who has always been willing to make things work for our clients. Maybe he'll have something available.

I hear Erin leave her office, her heels clicking on the hardwood floor. A moment later, she leans against my doorframe. I press send on the email.

'Nice hair,' she says as she takes a seat opposite my desk.

I run my hands through my poker-straight ends. 'Raf works wonders.'

Her tongue clicks. 'You think Raf would make time for me in the next few weeks?'

'I'm sure he'd find time to fit you in, shoot him a text.' I'm surprised she feels she has to ask me; Raf and Erin have always been close. I'd think he'd have her booked in before she'd even ask.

Erin hums in consideration, before she remembers what she came into my office for. 'We gotta book those tickets for the INFLUENCE awards. Like, now.'

'Shit, yeah.' Unsurprisingly, it's completely slipped my mind. The award ceremony is in less than a week, and we haven't organised a single thing. Quickly, I browse available flights to Sydney, find a time suitable and, upon checking Erin's calendar, book it.

'We should stay by the harbour,' Erin says, flicking through her phone for accommodation deals. Erin's always loved luxury, and I can hardly blame her. We grew up with so little, supported by a single mother. Still, booking accommodation looking over Sydney Harbour seems worthless when we'll be at an awards ceremony most of the night.

'I have a coupon after I had an awful stay last year,' she insists. 'Seriously. Let me book it.'

'All right,' I relent. Maybe we can enjoy the harbour views over breakfast.

Erin leans over to swipe my mocha and takes a sip. 'What are you going to do with Poppy? And Mouse?'

'Well,' I say and let the word hang between us. 'I was thinking of doing a terrible thing.'

Erin raises a brow. 'Which is?'

'Asking Jordan if he wanted to babysit.'

Erin stares at me blankly. 'Why would that be such a bad thing?'

'He's a client.'

'So?' Erin replies. 'He's a good kid, and he's almost out of the program.'

That is news to me. 'Really?'

'It's been six weeks, and he's hit almost all of his milestones. He's found a place to live, good work-life balance. I checked in with Laurie and she absolutely loves working with him.'

None of this should be surprising. The purpose of Jordan working with Erin was to get him back on his feet again, and I'm happy he's come so far in such a short time.

'So you don't think it'd be a bad idea?' I ask her. 'You know, professionally?'

Erin shakes her head. 'I don't see why not.'

My computer chimes as an email comes through. It's a reply from Ian, the real estate agent. I open it, but don't read past the first line: *sorry, A—nothing available for that budget.*

I groan, my head falling into my hands. Erin leans over the desk, peeping at the email. 'What is it?'

'I've been trying to find Mel a rental for the last two hours,' I say, falling back into my chair. 'We're working with her maximum budget, but there's nothing around.'

Erin turns the computer towards her to read the rest of the message. I don't mind; we share so much, there's nothing confidential between us.

'Ian's got a point here, you know,' she says, turning the computer back to me. 'There's a huge shortage of affordable housing, and no one is interested in leasing for below market value.'

'It's a human right, not a money-maker,' I mutter.

Most clients who come into Grace House don't have a secure home. Whether they're in the middle of divorce proceedings, experiencing homelessness or unable to find a suitable living situation for their needs; it's always the first and most crucial aspect of care we provide.

So when I hear things like 'a landlords market' and 'huge rental demand', I get a bit bitter.

'Why don't we offer housing?' Erin counters.

I scoff. 'You can't be serious.' But Erin looks completely serious with her brow furrowed slightly, and her lips a long, tense line.

'Erin, we can't just build apartments,' I say. 'We don't have that kind of money.'

'So, we'll find that kind of money. Donations. Fundraising,' she says, like rustling up the hundreds of thousands of dollars it would take to build apartments would be the simplest thing in the world.

It's a ridiculous idea. A complete pipe dream. Not only would we have to outbid investors to find a suitable property, but we'd also have to renovate the apartments, hire someone to manage the day-to-day administration, repair requests, rental payroll. Just the thought of starting a project like this is bringing on a headache.

'Erin, it's such a big idea. A huge project.'

'So?' Erin challenges. 'How good would it be to support people who need a rental short or long term? To have housing we can control.'

I shake my head, but she continues, 'and sure, we couldn't help everyone. We can't help everyone. But it would make a real difference to those we could.'

She has a point. Still, the thought of even considering this project is overwhelming. When we started Grace House, I'd always been happy to oversee the general operations and occasionally provide legal help to clients. Erin handled the social welfare, managed the clients and their needs.

Now we're staring down something neither of us has tackled before, and it's scary.

'Fine,' I say. 'We can do some investigating.'

I have no idea where we'll get the money, or how long this project is going to take, but as I glance back at the computer screen and the dozens of listings for apartments, I know Erin's right. This is something we need to do.

CHAPTER TEN

Out of all the gigs Erin's arranged for me—from the banjo tutoring, the shopping centre piano performances—the gig at Lavender Gardens is my favourite. It might not be the biggest gig of my career, but it feels like the most important. It feels like I'm making a difference.

Ana's mother, Grace, always attends my gigs. She's a sweet old lady who speaks English with a heavy Eastern European accent. Her fingers are knobbed and thin, but she has no problems working a crochet hook.

Rufus, another resident, claps as I walk into the sunroom with my guitar strapped to my back. Since I started, the nurses received a donated piano, but it needs a professional service to get it back to working function. Doesn't matter. The guitar suits me nicely.

A few of the other residents walk into the sunroom as I set up to play. I see Grace in the corner of the room. She's working on a blanket; her fingers moving the crochet hook with practiced ease. She looks up at me and smiles. I don't think she knows my name, but she knows why I'm here.

I'm playing more than I ever have—I have multiple gigs a week—but I have written nothing in months. At Lavender Gardens, I only sing covers. Things the folks know that brighten their spirits. Remind them of times gone by. Occasionally, I'll get inspiration in the early hours of the morning and my fingers will itch to play something, but I risk waking Talia up.

After the set, I grab my phone from my satchel. There's a message from Marco: *wanna hang at mine?*

Sure, just finishing up a gig, I type back. *Come over now?*

On Bourke St? Marco asks as I slip my guitar back into its case. *Yeah, swing by whenever.*

Bourke Street is the crème de la crème of gigging locations for wannabe musicians and celebrities doing down low gigs. Music producers pluck talent off the literal street.

Nah, I reply. *Private function.*

Marco doesn't need to know it's a retirement village. He always keeps his projects under wraps, citing 'contractual obligations'. It's about time I did the same.

I take the tram into the city and switch at Flinders Street station, grabbing a six pack of beer before continuing to Marco's place. Marco lives in a town-house in Brunswick; the door's half-open when I walk through the rusty gate. The smell of weed and cigarette smoke lingers in the hall. I can hear Marco laughing in the courtyard past the kitchen and make my way out. He turns and smiles at me as I step through the screen door, a joint hovering over his lips.

'Jordie!' he drawls. 'You made it.' He gestures to the

three others in the courtyard, the smoke from his blunt following his hand. 'This is Lissy, Jade and Shawn.'

'We've met,' Shawn says. He's sitting on the edge of a bare garden bed, rolling a joint on the brick. The girls are lounging on beach towels, soaking up the rare autumn sun. One looks out from under her glasses at me, but otherwise they don't talk.

'How was your gig?' Marco takes a long drag of the joint before passing it to me.

'Good.' I take a puff of the joint, not letting it in my lungs, before handing it to one of the girls.

'Thanks,' she smiles and smokes, a long stream of smoke billowing from her nostrils a second later.

I crack a beer and find a seat beside Shawn. 'What have you been doing?'

Marco shrugs lazily. 'Did a bit of writing.' He leans over to take the joint from Lissy. 'Most of it was a bit shit.'

'It needs work,' Shawn replies. 'But some of it's good.'

Marco shakes his head, annoyance flashing over his face. Ever since he got the record deal, he's been hard on himself, on his music. Everything's riding on this album. This is his shot.

Shawn turns to me. 'How's your writing?'

'Not good,' I admit. 'I haven't been able to write anything decent in a while. Housing issues. Unemployment.'

'Sometimes you just have to let yourself write shit,' Shawn says. 'But I get it. Some of the best stuff comes after the hard times.'

Marco huffs from his seat opposite us. 'Jordie's just playing poor,' he says, venom on his tongue.

Shawn doesn't say anything, and I'm too stunned to speak.

Marco continues. 'His family is fucking loaded. He chooses to be poor to make better art.'

'That's not true,' I say before I can stop myself. Angry and drunk, Marco flicks the end of his joint at me, and it hits my ankle. Hurts like a bitch.

'Any time he wants, he can run back to the bank of Mum and Dad,' Marco drawls. 'Whenever shit gets too hard, he's got a safety net.'

I hadn't realised how drunk Marco was when I walked in; how frustrated he was with his own work. Now he's lashing out.

'Fuck you,' I say, getting up. 'I don't have to put up with this shit.'

'Yeah, fuck me,' Marco slurs.

I push past him and go back into the house, grabbing my guitar and beers. I'm glad I didn't smoke too much because it would have been an awful high.

The next day, I spend a few hours in the library editing an assignment before grabbing a one-dollar coffee from Coles Express.

I see a poster for the composition prize with the words CLOSING SOON in big bold print.

When I get home, Talia's leaving for work. She says a quick goodbye as she rushes out the door. I linger in the kitchen, scarfing down a falafel wrap before grabbing my guitar and heading out into the courtyard. The smell of late flowering marigolds hangs the air. It's a beautiful, sunny day, but rain clouds linger on the horizon.

Fuck Marco.

I'd gone to bed angry. Angry at him. Angry at his words. Angry at how he'd weaponised our friendship, at everything I gave him.

I'd thought maybe he'd text me this morning; want to apologise, but I haven't heard from him. Maybe he's still drunk.

Without thinking, I begin plucking away on the guitar, cycling through clusters of notes until I find something that sticks. Occasionally, I stop to scribble something down. A few notes become a page; a page becomes two. The streetlamps flicker on, but it's not too cold yet, so I spend a little bit longer writing. As the first spittle of rain hits my cheek, I have the beginnings of what could be a song scribbled out across five pages in my notebook.

It's a start, at least.

I grab my phone from the kitchen bench. There's a message from my sister, Megan, asking what I'll get Mum for her birthday in three weeks' time and if I'm thinking about coming back to Sydney.

Sydney's the last place I want to be, but I don't want to tell Megan that. I also don't have the money. I don't want to tell Megan *that* either; she'll pity me and send me the cash.

Probs get her a voucher, I reply to Megan. *Class is hectic atm, can't make it home.*

It's a lie but she'll likely believe it.

I grab a beer from the fridge and flick on the TV. Talia isn't due home until the morning, so I have the place to myself. There's half of a pizza in the fridge I can heat up whenever I want.

For the first time in a long time, it feels like I can actually breathe.

On Wednesday, I meet with Erin. She seems distracted, which isn't normal for her. Normally she's organised, cool and collected. Today, her hair is up in a messy bun and she's chewing her lip.

'How are things?' I say, trying to break this weird tension between us. She looks up from my file and smiles politely.

'Busy,' she admits. 'Ana's been stressed, so in turn, I've been stressed.'

I'm surprised she mentioned Ana, or the reason behind her stress. But just as she says it, the mask returns. Erin puts down her coffee and pulls up my file.

'So, place of our own? check!' she says. 'How's university?'

'Good. I just submitted another assignment.'

She nods. 'Passing grades? Check!' she looks at me over her glasses. 'Work?'

'Two steady shifts a week at the café.'

She types my response into the computer. 'Nice. And the gigs?'

'Still going strong. The banjo kid's making good progress.'

She snorts with laughter. 'We need more banjo players. It's such a happy instrument.' She types something else into her computer and then turns back to me. 'So, you're feeling good?'

I nod. 'Yeah.' It's an honest answer. Marco and his shitty comments aside, I feel like things are finally coming together. 'I feel good. Better than I did.'

'I think you're doing really well,' Erin says. 'In fact, I don't think you need our help much longer. It feels like you've really got a grasp of things now.'

Panic floods through me. 'Are you sure?'

Erin looks back at her computer screen. 'We know that when clients meet their markers, they have an eighty percent chance of not returning to assisted help. You've flown through your markers and hit your milestones.' She gives me a kind smile. 'But if you do just want someone to talk to, or if you need support in the future, we'll be here.'

'So that's it?' I ask. 'I'm free?'

Erin scoffs. 'Don't make it sound so bad. This is a good thing. Does it not feel like a good thing?'

I force a smile. 'No, it's a good thing.'

Erin sees straight through it. Damn her and her incredible skill at reading social cues. 'We'll always be here if you need us.'

'I appreciate that, thanks.' Standing up, I reach out to shake Erin's hand. Her grips surprisingly hard.

'Take care, Jordan,' she says. 'Also, Ana wanted to see you. I think she's still in her office if you want to head down.'

My hands start to sweat. 'Right,' I say, trying to keep my voice even. I grab my satchel and head down the hallway. Ana's door is slightly open, and I can hear her typing.

A thought pops up, cliché like a lightbulb in a children's cartoon.

Now that I'm not her client, I could ask her out.

But too much time has passed since we went axe-throwing, I know she's at a comfortable distance. She's put *me* at a comfortable distance.

As I come to her office door, I inject myself with a fake confidence. Be someone bigger, more confident than you are—make her want you.

'Jordan!' she says brightly as I knock on the door. 'How are you?'

It's the first time I've seen her in weeks. She's had a haircut and her hair falls in perfect curls around her shoulders. Her smile is like looking in the sun on a warm spring afternoon, almost blinding in its brilliance.

'I'm good.' Stupid response. Lame. My clothes are suddenly too hot. 'How are you?'

'Good,' she replies. She rises from her chair. Her navy dress hugs her hips and thighs, the cut of her blazer cinching her waist. 'Since you're not a client anymore...'

'Yes?' I say. Maybe I won't have to do all the work; maybe she's been waiting for this as much as I have.

'Would you be interested in babysitting?' she finishes.

For a moment, I'm not sure I heard correctly. 'Babysitting?' I parrot.

'It'd only be for a night. Erin and I have an awards ceremony on this Saturday in Sydney. We'd be back by midday Sunday, at the latest.'

To be honest, I hadn't expected *this*. I'm not exactly experienced with kids. The only other kid in my life is my niece, Julia, and Megan always had highly trained nannies to look after her the nights she and her husband were away.

She must read the apprehension on my face. 'You don't have to. I can always find someone else.'

The way her voice trails off makes it clear that it's going to be difficult finding someone else; that she'd hoped I'd say yes. And hell, if I planned on dating Ana, of course Poppy would be involved. This is my chance to get to know her.

'I'd love to.'

Ana smiles but it's clear she doesn't believe me. 'Really?'

'Yeah, it'll be fun.' Maybe not my ideal Saturday night 'fun' but it'll be fun, nonetheless. 'I assume we'll get money for pizza.'

Ana laughs. 'Yes, there'll be money for pizza.' She looks at me with an expression I can't quite explain, somewhere between disbelief and relief. 'Thank you,' she says genuinely. 'I really mean that.'

I shrug. 'I'm happy to help.'

The phone in my pocket chimes; I already know it's the reminder to leave for piano tutoring. Ana raises an eyebrow. 'Email you the details?'

I nod. 'Yeah, sounds good.'

CHAPTER ELEVEN

It's Wednesday, 4:39am, when I get the first shitty text.

My phone vibrates on my bedside. I reach for it blearily, fumbling with the button to the lock screen until it shines white hot light into my unprepared cornea.

Jon's words appear on the screen.

When can we tell her I'm her dad?

I read it twice, once with one eye, and then with two, until I'm half-propped up in bed, wondering at quarter to five in the morning where men get the audacity—

Jon Willoughby takes my kid to the park one time in four years, and suddenly thinks he has the right to be called 'dad'. Next, he'll be asking me to change her last name.

I need a coffee. Now that I'm awake—and enraged —I walk into the kitchen, feed Mouse and run a coffee. Since the mishap with Poppy a few weeks ago, I've moved my coffee machine into the toaster nook.

After a few sips of my latte, I feel like I'm in a

better state of mind to text Jon. Best to do it now, lest it hang over my workday.

When she's old enough to understand, I write back. *And you're a consistent figure in her life.*

Jon texts right back. That's a bad sign. He's probably drunk.

I told you I want to be that.

Well, actions speak louder than words, Jon.

And then the kicker. He writes, *I want to be a family again.*

I stare at that message for a long time. Truthfully, I don't know what to think. Does he mean what I think he means? Or does he just want to show up for Poppy? The thought is both terrifying and completely overwhelming. Six weeks ago, he wasn't a part of my life. Now he's here. Asking for things he let go of years ago. Poppy and I are fine without him.

And yet, I know I can't deny my daughter a relationship with her father. I'd be lying to myself if I said I hadn't wished Jon would want a relationship with Poppy. That he'd change his mind.

I put my phone down, grab a fresh towel, and take a shower. Jon can wait. As I towel my hair dry, I hear Poppy playing in her room; it's still quite early so I'm surprised she's awake. When I pop my head in, I see that she's playing in a game in her dollhouse.

For a second, I stop and watch her play. I don't interrupt her. I don't berate her for being up so early or tell her to get dressed and prepare for the day. Instead, I just watch.

Whatever games she's playing, she's completely engrossed. She mutters dialogue as the dolls decide on what to order for breakfast. Then, they take a seat at a table and Poppy takes their order. I leave then, afraid she'll turn and see me peeking through the doorway and break the spell of early childhood.

The second shitty text comes through on Friday at 7:10pm. I don't read it right away because I'm having dinner with Jon. After the ordeal yesterday, I thought it'd be better to meet and discuss our differences of opinion.

We're at an Italian place in Carlton, which is only a few blocks away from the room he's renting while in Melbourne. It's a nice place; small and cosy. The bartenders murmur amongst themselves while polishing the glasses, catching my eye as I raise my hand to order another glass of wine.

Jon sits across the table. He's gelled his hair back, shining in the dim candlelight. He wears a cream linen button-down shirt, black jeans and far too much cologne. It's like he's come from an audition for Grease.

He's halfway through telling me how much it would mean to him if we went up to Sydney once every six months as the waiter deposits another generously poured glass of wine in front of me.

'I know she's too young to fly on a plane by herself, but if we timed it with when you come to Sydney for business, why not bring her along?'

'Look,' I say to Jon. 'I'm not saying that it can't happen, but—'

'Good, because—'

'Let me finish.' I refuse to be spoken over. 'We need to acknowledge that you have had zip to do with Poppy's life since she was born. Since *before* she was born.' Jon's face changes immediately. His brow furrows; his mouth a tight white line. 'The first few years were hard, Jon. You weren't there for any of them. I'm still angry about that.'

'You're going to deny me access to my daughter because you're angry?' he immediately retorts.

I hate how he twists my words. He's always done it. One small criticism and he flies off the handle.

'I didn't say that, and you know it.' I refuse to be manipulated by this man. 'Now you come back into our lives when Poppy and I are in a good place. You want us to travel to Sydney when you've not said when you'll come back to Melbourne? When you'll be doing things to see Poppy. When you'll make an effort.'

Jon looks at me sourly. 'I feel you're shutting me out, Ana.'

'I'm saying that you're the one who needs to put effort into being in Poppy's life. Not me.'

'That's what I'm trying to do,' he says, clearly exasperated. 'And every time I suggest something, you shoot me down.'

'That's because you're asking *me* to do it, Jon. You're asking me to come to Sydney. You're asking me to do things so you can see our daughter.'

'You're just going to make me jump through hoops,' he snaps back. 'You won't even let her call me Dad. She deserves to know.'

'Why do you always bring that up?' It comes out without thinking and immediately I wish I had said nothing. Jon's face hardens. I can almost see his walls going up; the cogs in his brain whirl as he thinks of what he can say that will hurt me just as much as I've hurt him.

How did I find myself back in this toxic cycle?

'I'm not saying she'll never know,' I continue. 'At the start of the year, she came home from preschool with a family tree. She asked me then. I said nothing because I knew as soon as I did she'd want to know why you weren't here.' My throat's burning, and I cough to clear it. 'Why are her classmate's mum and dad separated, but her classmate still sees her dad on the weekend? How do you tell a four-year-old their father abandoned her?'

Jon stares at me blankly. We haven't even ordered, but I realise I'm done with this dinner. With this conversation. Done with the way Jon makes me feel. Like a terrible mother and a bad person.

'I can't do this anymore, Jon.' Standing, I grab my coat and my purse.

'Ana, wait,' he says.

I shake my head, throwing a twenty-dollar note down onto the table and shouldering on my coat.

His hand grips my arm. It's not a tight grip, but the intention's there. Control. 'Don't leave.'

'Let me go, Jon.'

He looks down at his hand as if he's not realised what he's done. He lets me go.

'Why now?' I ask. It's the only question he hasn't answered. 'Why now, of all times?'

He shrugs. 'I saw a photo of you online, some event you were at. Got me thinking.'

I've heard enough. 'Goodbye, Jon.'

This time, he doesn't protest. I step out onto the street. It's cold and windy, but I steel myself and walk towards the cab rank at the end of the block. By the time I reach it, the walk has revitalised me and I decide to continue onto the tram stop.

I don't remember the last time I took a tram.

Maybe to the footy. When I first moved here, I used to take trams all the time. Jon and I would take them to work, to the supermarket, to the laundromat to wash our clothes.

The tram rocks as it makes its way into the city. I press my forehead against the cool glass and watch the city pass me. As my anger simmer, my stomach grumbles and I realise I've only had two glasses of wine for dinner. At Flinders Street Station, I pull out my phone to order a burger, only to be greeted by two missed calls from Jon and the forgotten message from Erin.

Call me when you can.

Shit.

She's been watching Poppy. Immediately, I think something's wrong.

I board my next tram, my stomach in my throat, and call Erin as soon as I'm seated.

'Please don't tell me you're in hospital,' I say as soon as she picks up. We're flying to Sydney for the award ceremony tomorrow; I cannot deal with a hospitalisation now.

'We're not at the hospital,' Erin replies. 'But you're not gonna like this.'

I brace myself. 'What is it?'

'Poppy and I have nits.'

Nits. Well, she's been at preschool for almost six months. Since she's been to daycare, we've had hand, foot and mouth disease, we've had pneumonia, and a narrowly missed a round of chickenpox.

We were due for nits.

'How bad is it?' I ask.

'Burn the apartment down bad,' Erin replies. 'I feel them moving, Ana. Are you sure you're not infected?'

The urge to itch comes over me. 'I'll have to check. I think I'm fine.'

'Raf found them. He put us in nit quarantine. Like I haven't had enough of that word,' Erin huffs. 'He's coming around tomorrow to de-nit us both.'

'I'm so sorry, Erin. I had no idea.' Everything I need to do runs through my head. I'll have to call the preschool and let them know; wash Poppy's bedsheets, her pillowcase, her hats...

Erin continues. 'I won't be able to go to Sydney. Would you be okay going by yourself?'

Shit. The award ceremony. The thought of going alone makes me want to go straight over to Erin's place and get myself infested.

I scoff. 'Honestly, what are the chances we even get the award?'

'But I know you've been looking forward to going,' Erin replies. 'And you got that dress tailored. You should go. Have fun.'

'It's not fun without you,' I say. It's the truth. We'd planned the weekend together. Even booked that stupid hotel by the harbour.

'Why don't you ask Jordan to go?'

The question is so random; I have to make sure I've heard her correctly. 'Jordan?'

'He was babysitting Poppy, wasn't he? Plus, he was a client, and he probably has connections in Sydney he'd recognise at the gala. It's *all* about networking.'

I hate that it's such a good idea.

'I think it's a great idea,' Erin says as if reading my mind.

'Of course, you do,' I mutter. Not for the first time, I wonder if Erin suspects there is something —or the glimmer of something—between Jordan and I. I've never told her about the drink we got; but she's always been intuitive. Maybe she's figured it out on her own. 'What if he says no?'

'Then we tell INFLUENCE that some creative infectious disease ravaged our office, and we can't make it.'

'Gross,' I reply.

Maybe it would be a good idea to invite him. Sydney is his old stomping ground after all. He'd have recommendations for good places to eat and things to do. It'd be nice not to face the award ceremony alone.

We fly out on tomorrow morning. If I'm going to ask him, I need to do it tonight.

'I'll ask him,' I resolve. 'As soon as I wash Poppy's bedsheets. And her towels.'

'And her hairbrush,' Erin adds. 'Make sure you put her hairbrush in boiling water.'

'Great.' Might as well clean the entire apartment. I pause. 'Can cats get nits?'

CHAPTER TWELVE

When Ana called me at nine-thirty and asked if I had any plans tomorrow, I'd thought I was dreaming. Rain was falling outside, gently smacking on the stone pavement. My bedroom was lit with the cool light of the streetlamp, curtains open, my guitar lying next to me like a lover. I didn't remember falling asleep. Hearing my ringtone and seeing Ana's name flash up on the screen had felt like a dream.

Now we're waiting to board our flight to Sydney in the business lounge. Ana drinks coffee opposite me, her eyes focusing on her phone.

'So,' Ana says. 'I suppose we should go through the agenda for the weekend?'

I sip my coffee. 'Sure.'

"I've got a suit fitting lined up at eleven. Then a haircut and facial shave at twelve. Lunch at one, then we check into the hotel room where we'll get ready.'

'Haircut and shave?' I echo. I didn't realise she'd arrange anything for me. 'And don't worry about a suit fitting. I have like a hundred. My sister can courier one over.'

Ana's lip twitches. I suppose she doesn't like her plans changing. 'Well, we will still need to swing by to pick up my dress. The dinner officially starts at six, but we'll have to navigate peak hour traffic, so even though it's just on the other side of the city, we'll have to leave at five.'

'It won't take us an hour to get across the city.' This minute-by-minute play is doing my head in. I had no idea Ana was so by the books. So committed to her schedule. 'Why aren't we staying at the same hotel as the awards?'

'My sister arranged a room in Darling Harbour before she found out she couldn't come.' She shakes her head, indicating it is a whole *thing* she doesn't really want to get into.

'Right,' I say. I get the sense that Ana finds comfort in her planners, in her schedule, so I don't push it. It's clear this weekend is already off to a bad start. 'So, what happened to Erin?'

The ghost of a smile touches Ana's lips. 'Poppy gave her nits.'

That's... not what I expected.

'Don't worry,' Ana continues. 'I'm fine. Clean.'

As we rise through the air, Ana flicks through a well-worn paperback. I fidget nervously, gazing out the porthole window as Melbourne disappears below us. I've never been a nervous flyer, but I don't feel comfortable. The seats are so small that our thighs are touching, and no amount of squirming in my seat will prevent it. Plane seats aren't made for someone like me. Ana pretends not to notice it.

It's sunny in Sydney when we land. A slap in the face to Melbourne's dreary late-May weather. People walk the streets in short-sleeved t-shirts, eat their lunch alfresco. My stomach rumbles as the taxi drops us off near Pitt Street, and we step out onto a row of cafes, restaurants, and bars. There's so much variety, so much to choose from, you could spend a week roaming the length of Pitt Street for your every meal and still not eat your way through it.

'Time for a coffee?' I suggest, as I throw my duffel bag over my shoulder.

'Sure,' Ana replies as she steps out of the taxi. 'But not too long.'

We find a small cafe where we can sit just off Pitt Street. The CBD is littered with construction and everyone's in a rush. Even Ana's checking her watch as we wait to order.

'Go halves in a...,' I scan the refrigerator by the counter. 'Hazelnut, quinoa and cacao protein slice?'

It's the least gross option in a fridge full of gross. What's so wrong with a blueberry muffin?

Ana stifles a laugh. 'Sure.'

We order our coffee and find a seat towards the back of the cafe. Outside, a jackhammer starts up, it's hammering only adding to the uniquely chaotic ambience a café on Pitt Street can offer. Ana sits opposite me and picks up her phone.

'Is Poppy okay?' I ask.

She looks up and gives a bashful smile. 'Just checking in. Erin might be awake by now. Last night was the big delousing.'

'Gross.'

Ana nods in agreement. 'Glad it's her and not me.'

The barista brings our coffees to the table, and I

inhale. God, I love the smell of coffee. The warmth. The fullness of it. It smells like rainy autumn afternoons, and early summer mornings when you rise before the sun's up because it's too damn hot to stay in bed. I love the sound of the coffee machine running, drinking out of my favourite mug.

The barista places the protein slice between us and I break it in half, giving her the bigger piece.

Ana brings her latte to her lips absentmindedly, her gaze focused on her phone. Then, she takes a bite of her slice. Finally, when she's finished checking in on her sister, she slips her phone back in her bag. There's a small crumb of protein slice on her upper lip.

'Um,' I say.

'What?' she asks, her brow furrowing.

'You have a bit of, um, protein slice on your upper lip.' I place my finger on my own lip, indicating where the crumb is.

She laughs and brushes it off. 'Thank you. I know it's healthy and all that, but how does this place not have a single muffin? You know when it's two o'clock on an awful day, you just want something full of carbs and sugar.'

'Growing up in Vaucluse, the closest Maccas is on Bondi Beach.' I chew on the protein slice. It's a bit rubbery. 'I always smuggled it home from the city after school.'

Ana raises a brow. 'Vaucluse? Fancy.'

I hum. 'It was. Mum and Dad still live there.'

'You don't feel like visiting them?'

'We'll meet Megan tonight,' I say. 'And she's already agreed to courier the suit over, but seeing my dad is the last thing I want to do.'

A strange expression crosses Ana's face: something

I can't decipher. She nods. 'It'll be nice to meet your sister.'

We finish the coffee and walk down Pitt Street Mall. Even in the early morning, the strip is busy. We weave through crowds of people, navigating towards a lift at the base of the building. I'm glad to get out of the street. Almost six million people live in Sydney, but I still feel like I'm going to run into someone I don't want to see. It's a silly feeling, but I can't shake it.

'Allegra is an old friend,' Ana says as she punches the button for the seventh floor. It's a relief to be off the street, but as the elevator doors opens to a sweeping bridal and evening boutique, the fear returns. The shop floor is littered with brides, their entourages, and racks and racks of gowns.

It's the kind of place that serves champagne on arrival, so when a woman in a tight-fitting black dress appears from the register, I'm not surprised when she says, 'Ana! Champagne?'

Ana laughs and gives the woman an air kiss. 'Not this time, Allegra.'

Allegra looks at her, unconvinced. 'An espresso martini?'

'I'm just here to pick up my dress.'

Allegra clicks her tongue in disapproval and disappears to fetch Ana's dress. I watch a bride model a large puffy dress to onlookers, who beam with happiness. I notice they've caught Ana's attention too; and she regards the group with a cool, mellow expression. I wonder if Ana's ever been married, but it seems wrong to ask her. Too personal.

Allegra returns with a large, zipped black dress bag. 'Enjoy, my dear,' she says as she hands the bag to Ana. 'Now, for your friend?'

Her eyes turn to me, and it feels like she's sizing up her next meal.

'Jordan actually has his suit sorted,' Ana intervenes. 'So we won't need to try on anything today.'

Allegra's face drops slightly. 'Well, that's a bit of fun taken out of my day. You know I love dressing men.' She gives Ana a smile. 'Until next time, dear.'

As we leave the boutique, I count myself lucky that past-me was savvy enough to leave a few boxes of clothes in Megan's basement. The last thing I want to do is play dress up.

'Guess we should go to the hotel to drop this off,' Ana says, checking her watch. 'Then, we have a bit of time before the barber appointment, so I guess we can—,'

'I want to take you somewhere,' I interrupt.

Ana looks at me, thrown off. 'Where?'

'Trust me.'

'No,' she says immediately. 'No, I don't have time for this. Where?'

'We'll have the time,' I assure her as we step out into Pitt Street Mall. Grabbing my phone from my pocket, I order us a ride. Luckily, there's a slew of cars meandering around the CBD. The app assigns a car a minute away. 'Come on. We'll drop the dress on the way.'

A black Hyundai pulls into a taxi rank and waves for us to get in. Ana slides into the backseat beside me, her jaw clenched.

'Two stops,' I say, adding the second stop to the app. 'Thanks, mate.'

The driver nods and waits until it's safe to re-join traffic. 'Music?' he asks.

'No thanks,' I say, just as Ana says: 'That'd be great.'

He looks between us in the rear vision mirror. 'Which one?'

'Music's fine,' I reply as Ana says: 'We can keep it off.' She looks at me, clearly unamused. First, I've hijacked the schedule for the day and now I'm arguing with her over music. To be fair, it needed to be hijacked. Time is meant to be enjoyed, wasted, and not segmented or made productive and purposeful every minute of every day of every week. All we gotta do is get to the award ceremony by six, but it's a Saturday. We gotta live a little.

'I decide for you,' the driver replies and hits a button on the stereo. The radio plays, but it's a talk-back show. Not even music.

As we pull up at the hotel, I take Ana's dress and run it inside. She gives me a glare as I slip back into the car.

'You'll like it,' I promise as the driver sets off again. 'It'll be fun.'

Ana opens her mouth but must think better of whatever she wants to say.

'What? Didn't schedule time for fun?'

'*Tonight* will be fun.' Something in her tone tells me she's lying. And she knows it.

'Stuffy award ceremonies and talking shop with my politician sister? Real fun weekend planned.' Out the window, the blue of the sea peeps through the rows of luxurious houses. If we wound down the window now, the briny sea air would flood through the car.

The driver pulls up on a street lined with gangly salt bushes. Ana steps out of the back seat and breathes deeply. She looks at me, a smile playing on her lips. 'You brought us to the beach?'

'My old beach.' I motion for us to walk up the

street. It's always been eerily silent in Vaucluse; the streets are quiet save for the odd-dog walker. Just how the residents like it. We make our way up the hill that looks down to Dove Beach, and the ocean comes into view. Ana lingers near the peak.

'My old stomping ground,' I say as we come to a stop.

'I can imagine you playing *Wonderwall* down there. Impressing the girls.'

I laugh because it's true. 'Come on. There's a great smoothie place around the corner.'

The small beachside shops aren't busy at this time of day; two older ladies sit by the beachside cafe drinking lattes and staring out onto the ocean. A salty breeze ruffles the hem of their dresses, the set curls of their hair.

The shops at Vaucluse aren't like what you'd find at a normal beach; the greasy fish-and-chip shop has been replaced by a trendy smoothie shack. There's a gourmet restaurant that books out weeks in advance over summer. There's no little surf wear shop, no fishing tackle in freezer boxes. The rents are far too high, and too much commercialism would attract tourists. These beaches might as well be private to the residents of the surrounding suburbs.

The little smoothie shop is still open; it's menu seasonal and super expensive. Anna orders the 'Green Goddess' smoothie and I get one called 'Coco-Nutty'.

'How many girls have you taken to this little smoothie shop?' Ana asks as we wander down to the beach. She slides off her shoes and smiles as the sand touches her toes. I do the same, shoving my socks into my sneakers.

'Too many to count,' I reply, and she laughs.

We find a place on the firm sand and sit, watching the waves roll in. There's a gentle swell today; Dove Beach curls around the southern point of Sydney Harbour, and the marshes and islands protect the inner beaches from the harsh waves.

'Thanks for bringing me here. I don't remember the last time I went to the beach,' she says. 'With work, and,' she waves her hand. 'Everything.'

I don't really know what 'everything' means. I'm about to ask, but then Ana looks at me and says, 'Should we get in?'

'The water?' I say dumbly.

She stands up to shuck off her blazer. 'Yeah. Why not?'

'It's winter?'

Ana shrugs as she pulls her shirt up over her head and holy shit. Something in my brain just stops as I see her lacy black bra. 'Not as cold as Melbourne.' She gives me a challenging look. 'Come on.'

'Ugh, fine.' I suck down the rest of my smoothie and pull off my hoodie and shirt. As I undo the belt of my jeans, Ana runs forward in her black underwear set, her feet touching the waves.

I kick off my jeans and run after her. Going for a dip wasn't exactly what I had in mind, but

I'm not about to back out.

Ana's swum out deeper by the time my toes touch the edge of the water. It's not as cold as I thought it would be until a wave slaps against by bare thighs and I resist the urge to scream. Ana laughs, her voice echoing through the inlet.

I swim out to meet her, dunking my head under a wave.

'Ugh, I miss the ocean,' she says as I reach her. Her hair is an inky shadow around her shoulders as she lies back in the water and just *floats*.

A few hundred metres away, a small ferry transports passengers to the port at the mouth of the harbour; the very peak of Watsons Bay. The boat's chugging generates waves, and we ride the peak and troughs of the sudden swell. A wave crests and goes over our heads. I dive under, coming up to wipe the stinging salt water from my face. Ana resurfaces, laughing and loose-footed. She leans against me, and on instinct I grab her. My hand slips around her waist and I pull her to stand.

She pushes her hair back and giggles. Sea water drips off the end of her nose, lingers on her bottom lips. I can't look away.

'Should we go in?' she asks breathlessly.

I glance back at our stuff on the beach. We didn't bring a towel or anything. 'We better. Check the time.'

Ana scoffs. 'Like you didn't throw my schedule out the window.'

'It needed to be thrown out the window,' I challenge.

Ana hums and pushes off me to head back to shore. We splash our way back to the beach, take our clothes and find a space on the lawn-covered hill to dry off. It's not as uncomfortable as I thought it would be but the sun feels nice on my skin. The breeze is gentle and warm; at least compared to Melbourne. I'm sure it's scandalous to the residents of Vaucluse; two scantily-dressed outsiders relaxing near the beach in their knickers but fuck 'em.

Beside me, Ana lets out a relaxed sigh.

'We should go,' she says.

I reach out, find her hand. Her fingers are cold. 'We can stay a little longer.'

I expect her to rebuff me. To grab her clothes and get redressed, but instead she laces her fingers between mine and settles down. Guess we can.'

CHAPTER THIRTEEN

'There must be some mistake,' I say to the young girl behind reception. Her perfectly manicured fingers fly across the keyboard.

'Not a mistake, ma'am,' she replies. Her dark, long-lashed eyes flick to me and then to Jordan, who is loitering in the lobby behind me. 'The reservation your sister made is for a queen room.'

Erin and I are close, but we're not *that* close. She wouldn't have booked a queen bed on purpose.

But even if Erin was here, we could have made the situation work. It's not the first time we would have shared a bed. I turn to look at Jordan, who's leaning down to investigate fish in a large aquarium. This completely crosses the line.

I turn back to the receptionist. 'Is there anything else available? Could I purchase another room?'

Sympathy flashes across her face. 'I'm afraid not. There's a convention on. We've been booked out for weeks. I only secured this room on a cancellation.' She slides the key across the table. 'I'm very sorry for the mix-up, ma'am.'

I grab the key and turn it over in my hand. What am I going to say?

'It's fine,' I bite out, trying not to let my frustrations show. After all, this isn't her fault. But I don't know how I'm going to tell Jordan. Someone's gonna have to crash on the couch. 'Thank you.'

'Let me know if I can do anything else for you, ma'am,' she says earnestly.

I grab my suitcase and Jordan comes over, his suit slung over his shoulder and his duffel bag in his other hand. An elevator opens a few steps away.

'All good?' he asks as he steps into the elevator next to me. I press the button for the twelfth floor and the lift door closes. Twelfth floor? Maybe we'll have a view.

'Yeah,' I smile. 'Fine.'

It's two-thirty. We have three hours to dress for the awards ceremony and get a cab across the city. For the first time, nerves rip through my stomach. I never get nervous. But as I stand beside Jordan, so close I can smell his musky cologne, I feel overwhelmed.

This feels like a bad idea. But it's too late to back out now.

The elevator door opens, and we wander down a narrow hallway to our room. I prepare myself for the awkward conversation as the door swings open and I'm assaulted with the stench of strong floral deodoriser.

The room is, well, small.

Really small.

A large window showcases the beautiful Sydney cityscape; harbour bridge included. At least Erin got that right. In the far distance, the afternoon sun sparkles off the ocean. But nothing can draw our gaze away from the overly decorated queen bed sitting in the middle of a small room and the two wrapped chocolates lying innocently on the pillows.

'There's only one bed,' Jordan says. Opposite the offending bed, there's a large full-length mirror, a small desk, a strangely large TV and a well-stocked minibar. There's no couch. No pull-out.

I don't turn to look at him. I stare at the bed, wondering exactly how I ended up in this situation. Maybe if I continue to stare at it, the bed will miraculously break into two.

That's it.

I stalk forward and press my hand deep into the mattress, looking for the hidden seam. Sometimes, hotels push two singles together to save money. But no luck. We've been gifted a solid queen mattress.

'So, what do we do?' Jordan asks, standing in the hallway, his shoulder brushing against the doorframe.

There's no time to worry about who will sleep where. We need to get unpacked, showered, and ready to go.

'We can come back to this,' I wave my hand towards the bed, 'situation when we get back from the award ceremony. It's no big deal.'

'I could stay at my sister's,' he offers. 'I'm sure she wouldn't mind.'

'It's fine. We'll figure it out.' I grab a towel from the base of the bed. 'Now do you want first shower, or can I?'

The whole getting ready process is *infinitely* quicker

when a four-year-old is not involved. Jordan and I are showered, dressed, styled and ready within forty minutes flat. There's even time to get a drink at the hotel bar before ordering a car across town, Jordan convinces me.

'Ugh, the car's like twenty minutes away,' I mutter as we wait for our ride outside the hotel. I check my watch. At this rate, we're going to be at least ten minutes late. If not more with traffic. Why did I say yes to getting a drink? We could have been there by now.

Jordan's hand smooths over my shoulder. 'We'll get there. Don't stress.'

After showering, he'd gone to a barber down the road for a haircut. They'd tamed his frizzy blond curls into well-defined waves that transition into an excellent fade. He stands, hands in his pockets, looking nothing like the guy I found under the awning in the rain all those weeks ago.

'See,' he says, pulling me out of my daydream. He points to a car sliding into the driveway. 'Here they are.'

The car pulls into the curb and to my surprise, Jordan steps forward and opens the door for me.

'Thank you,' I say as I step down. Our eyes meet, and something runs through me, something electric.

'You're welcome,' he replies. Then he scoops down to grab my small train before shutting the door.

As we make our way across town, we hit traffic. It's inevitable, and we inch through the streets at a snail's pace. After twenty minutes, I briefly consider suggesting to Jordan we get out and leg it.

My phone chimes in my purse, and I fish it out.

Erin's sent me a message: a photo of Raf combing thick product through her hair.

You have no idea how gross this was, she writes underneath the caption.

I'm not talking to you, I shoot back.

What? Why?! What did I do?

The room you booked with your coupon was only a queen. And they're completely booked out.

Her response takes a minute to come through. *Oh shit, you're right. Sorry!!*

You will be sorry; I type back and then slip my phone back into my purse. My agitation at my sister is simmering under the surface, and I refuse to let it ruin a night I've looked forward to for the last few months.

Jordan's fingers drum on the door of the car. He's staring blankly out into the streets, completely zoned out.

'You okay?' I ask.

He snaps back to reality. 'Yeah. Of course. Just, um, nervous to see my sister. We still talk, but you know. I haven't seen her since I split from the family.'

'Is anyone else from your family going to be here tonight?' After all, INFLUENCE magazine is a leading women's publication, with a board and staff of high-profile women. If they're inviting the Premier of New South Wales, and she's actually showing up, surely more of Jordan's family are bound to be around.

'No, Dad hates functions that aren't about him,' he snickers. 'And Mum's social anxiety is too much these days. My other sisters live out of town.'

It's strange to hear about the Templetons outside of the national news. They always seem to be in the headlines; their lifestyles-of-the-rich-and-famous problems splashed across newspapers and social media. Tax evasion, cheating scandals, fights within the family. To hear about them in such domestic, intimate ways feels suddenly intrusive.

No wonder Jordan wanted to get out.

The taxi pulls up at the venue and I pay the fee— exorbitant, considering we barely travelled over five kilometres. Still, I was not about to jump on the tram in this gown.

Jordan takes a deep breath as the taxi departs. The warm sunlight hits his cheekbones, his cupid's bow, the curve of his brow.

I nudge my shoulder with his. 'You ready?'

'Yeah,' he clears his throat, his hands fidgeting with the hem of his suit. 'There's a lot of people here.'

'There are,' I confirm. Before I think better of it, I raise my hand and slip it into his.

He looks at me but doesn't say anything.

I squeeze his hand. A silent message.

He squeezes back.

We're sat at a table with lovely people: a banker from Hobart, a marathon runner and her wife from Brisbane, and a social media influencer from Sydney. All very interesting people with very interesting stories.

Jordan sits beside me, his hand on my knee under the table. I'd thought it would feel weird, but it's strangely comforting. Megan, his sister, is on the podium a few metres away, giving the keynote address as the award ceremony officially kicks off. She's dressed in a beautiful emerald gown, her blonde hair cut bluntly at her shoulders. She speaks politely and civilly, and when she finally wraps up her speech, Jordan turns to me and says, 'You'd never know she hates public speaking.'

'She's the Premier,' I reply. 'Why get into politics?' Jordan opens his mouth, but I fill in the blanks before he responds. 'Let me guess: your dad had a guiding hand in it.'

'Bingo,' he chuckles before reaching forward to drain his drink. 'Another?'

'Sure,' I reply, because why the hell not? It's been a tough couple of months. Between Jon resurfacing and the whole thing with Greg Pryor, I just want to switch off. I just want to have fun.

The waiter hands me another glass of champagne as the editor-in-chief of INFLUENCE takes to the stage. But when Jordan's fingers begin absently stroking my inner knee, I can't think of anything else. My attention zones in on the lazy movements of his thumb and the weight of his hand on my knee. I think about what would happen if he dared skim them higher, how his warm palms would feel running up my inner thighs.

A round of applause snaps me out of my thoughts. The editor-in-chief finishes her speech and welcomes another woman onto the stage. It's Shelley. I recognise her from the photoshoot, though she's dyed her hair blonder in the weeks since. Behind her, someone wheels a table full of awards onto the stage.

Jordan's hand leaves my knee to clap. I instantly miss his touch.

I need to get a grip.

Shelley clears her throat and begins speaking. 'Tonight, we honour excellence in female entrepreneurship. The women who are striving forward and who are bringing others up with them. Our first award recognises a Leading Woman in a Business.'

Jordan leans in close. 'What category are you in, again?'

'And the winner is...' Shelley continues.

'Leading Woman in Not-For-Profit,' I answer in a hush.

'Eliza Wilkinson from Edward and Burton Solicitors!' Shelley announces. The room erupts into applause. A rowdy table to my left whistles and cheers. Eliza looks stunning as she takes to the stage for her award, her long black dress complimented by her stunning Aboriginal-flag earrings.

'This award means so much to me, thank you so much.' Her voice cracks towards the end of her speech. The crowd applauds as Eliza moves off the stage to celebrate with her table.

'Your award category is next,' Jordan says, his nose in the leaflet. 'You think you'll win?'

I've been trying not to think about it. The disappointment I know I'll feel if I don't win has never settled well with me, and I've been working on myself for weeks to lessen the blow. Maybe I'm just too competitive, but it feels shitty to compete with women being awarded for their work in the not-for-profit space, and even shittier to feel like I want to beat them.

'It's now my honour to announce the award for Leading Woman in a Not-For-Profit. Our first nomination is Aiko Yokohama from Dignity INC from Darwin. As the sustainability leader for Dignity, she's implemented a program that's led to an increase in biodegradable disposable nappies stocked in supermarkets.'

Cheers erupt from Aiko's table. Aiko sits in the

middle of her friends and colleagues, her face beet red. It must be nice to have that support.

As if reading my mind, Jordan takes my hand and squeezes it.

'You got this,' he whispers.

I don't think I do.

'The second nomination is Claudia Rosa-Hernandez from Rose Digital in Brisbane. As the CEO of Rose Digital, Claudia has increased the fundraising revenue of her clients to an excess of five million dollars and provides free coding and marketing courses to young women in underrepresented, regional and rural areas.'

I suck down the last sip of champagne. Who could compete with Claudia? Successful and altruistic? That woman has it all.

'Our final nominee is Ana Woods, CEO and CFO of Grace House in Melbourne. For the last four years, Grace House has helped thousands of at-risk people find safety and security by supporting them to find housing, employment and access health services.'

Jordan lets go of my hand to clap, whooping loudly. For a brief, horrifying moment, he's the only one who does so. I even think I hear Shelley laugh into the microphone. Slowly, though, a clap reverberates through the room, matching Jordan's energy.

'And the award goes to...,' Shelley pauses as she opens her golden envelope. Very gaudy. Surely, one can just use an iPad these days. 'Ana Woods of Grace House!'

Applause erupts from all around me. My body acts without my direction; I'm on autopilot as I rise out of my chair and walk towards the stage. Jordan gives me a broad smile, but I'm not sure if I smile back.

I get to the front of the stage, only to stop at the base of the staircase.

Of course, there would be steps. I'm not well-practiced in walking with heels and as I grab the railing, it wobbles under my hand. Great.

'Ana,' I hear my name called from the back of the room. I turn and see Jordan weaving his way through the crowd. 'Here, let me help.'

He stands beside the railing and holds out his hand. I look at him for a moment, dazed at the gesture and the realisation that under the bright lights of the stage, his blue eyes are stunning. With my hand in his, I ascend the staircase and cross the stage. Shelley kisses my cheek and whispers, 'congratulations'.

I take the award from her. Made of glass and strangely avocado-shaped, with a thick bottom and a rounded top, it's heavier than I thought it would be.

'Well,' I say into the microphone. 'This is certainly unexpected...'

CHAPTER FOURTEEN

Considering we're at best half-cut, Ana did a spectacular job with that speech. I wait for her at the base of the staircase and take her hand like I'm Prince Charming. Her eyes land on me and she smiles.

'Thank you,' she murmurs as she gets to the last step. Her gaze never wavers from mine.

'You're welcome,' I say. 'Cool trophy.'

She chuckles as we slip to the side of the room to make our way back to the table. Ana hands it to me and fuck, it's heavy. 'It's going straight to the pool-room,' she whispers.

We've almost made it back when I feel someone tug on the sleeve of my jacket. I stop, whirling around.

'I thought that was you by the stage,' Megan says. She gets up from her seat to pull me into a tight hug. She smells like Gucci perfume and the sweet-sour scent of prosecco on her breath. As I hug her back, I'm overwhelmed by how much I've missed her. I've missed her *so* much.

'I'm here with Ana,' I say. The complexity of our

relationship is far too much to boil down into a succinct introduction, so I simply say, 'She's a friend.'

Megan turns her attention to Ana. 'Congratulations on your award. It sounds like you do fantastic work.'

'Thank you so much.' Ana shakes Megan's hand, clearly a little starstruck. It's weird to think of Megan as a celebrity, but I guess she is. In a way that a socialite-turned-politician can be.

'She'd love to tell you more about it,' I say to Megan. 'What are you doing for breakfast tomorrow?'

Megan laughs. She can see right through what I'm doing, my clumsy attempt at networking. 'Sure. I'm having breakfast at home. Why don't you come through around eight? It's been a while since Julia's seen her uncle.'

Ana nudges me teasingly. 'You didn't tell me you were an uncle.'

Julia has her own Wikipedia sub-page, but it feels nice that Ana hasn't bothered to do her research on my family. Feels more authentic.

'The favourite uncle,' Megan confirms.

I scoff. 'The only uncle.'

Megan's phone rings on the table, and someone tries to get her attention.

'We'll see you at eight,' I reply. 'As long as this isn't some plan for me and Dad to have an intervention.'

'No Dad, I promise,' she says before picking up the phone. She gives us a silent little wave and then leaves to take the call in the hallway, her security close behind.

Waiters come around with more drinks as Ana plants her award the middle of our table like a damn centrepiece, much to the amusement of our tablemates.

The man beside her leans in close and whispers something in Ana's ear before slipping her a business card.

That's how it goes for the rest of the night: more and more people come up to Ana to pull her away, handing her business cards or asking for one in return. It's a whirl of networking with a liberal splash of alcohol. I hang back, not keen to steal her thunder or get recognised. Now and then, her eyes drift back to me. It feels more like emotional assurance than anything. That I'm still here; still hanging around but at around eleven, Ana makes eye contact with me and then nods towards the door.

She wants to go.

Back to the hotel with the one bed and no couch.

My back aches just thinking about spending the night on the floor.

I gather Ana's purse, making sure I have her phone and the award joining her on the other side of the room. Delicately, I extract her from the social bubble she's found herself in and we bid our goodbyes.

Outside, a line of cabs wait to take people across town. I go to flag one down, but then Ana pulls on my sleeve.

'Wait,' she slurs. 'Are you hungry?'

I can smell the champagne on her breath, and she's smiling. Ana is too serious to smile.

She's drunk.

Smashed, even.

'I could eat,' I admit. Dinner was a la carte and delicious, but no one would call the portion sizes huge. What are you thinking?'

'There's a Maccas a few blocks from here,' she says. 'I could *destroy* a burger right now.'

Maccas is exactly what I want right now. I look down at Ana's shoes. They're beautiful, but they're not practical. As if reading my mind, she reaches into her purse and pulls out a pair of fold-up flat shoes.

'For occasions like this!' she says. With her hand anchored on my shoulder, she slips off her heels and puts on the flats. Once she's balanced. Her arm loops in mine. I'm not sure if it's an intimacy thing or that she's so drunk she physically needs to lean on me. Either way, it's fine with me.

'Lead the way!' she commands.

'How many glasses did you have?' I ask as we begin to walk.

She shrugs. 'Hard to tell.'

It's an unseasonably warm night and the streets are busy; restaurants are full, and people spill out from bars and nightclubs. Heavy bass vibrates through the air. My blood feels electric in my veins, a mix of alcohol and adrenaline.

As soon as Ana sees the golden arch logo, she tugs me forward. We stumble towards the counter and Ana proceeds to order a small feast before fumbling out her card and slapping it down on the EFTPOS machine.

'You wanna go back to the hotel and eat these in the bed?' she asks as we wait.

'The one bed we have?'

'Oh my god, the one bed,' she laughs. 'I'm so sorry. I didn't know.'

'It's fine,' I assure her. 'If it's fine with you.'

She grins, playfulness dancing in her eyes. "It's fine with me.'

Her body presses against mine; I'm not sure if it's purposeful or just a sway. I look down at Ana and she looks up at me before cuddling in closer. Definitely purposeful, then. Her dark eyes flick down to my lips and then up again; and God damn if I don't want to kiss her right now.

'Order fifty-five!' the server calls.

'That's us!' Ana says, stumbling away from me. She grabs the bags and drinks from the server like it's a prize. 'Let's go.'

We find a cab on the street and direct it back to the hotel, fumbling to put our seatbelts on in the back. Ana rifles through the takeaway bag and pulls out a single chip. Swooping in, I snatch the chip from her fingers with my teeth.

'Jordan, you thief!' she complains as she rifles through the bag again. This time, she grabs a chicken nugget and eats it in one bite.

The taxi pulls into our hotel a few moments later and dumps us on the corner, clearly glad to have gotten rid of us. Drunk and laughing, we make our way to our hotel room, careful not to leave a trail of chips behind us.

'Home sweet home,' Ana says as she pushes off her dress and slips into the bed in her underwear and bra.

I hesitate at the doorway, unsure if I'm allowed to join her, but then she snorts. 'Come on, food's getting cold.'

Don't need to be told twice. I take off my shoes and jacket before jumping in beside her.

'Your drink, sir,' she says in an old-timey accent, handing me a paper cup full of coke.

'Thank you, my lady,' I parrot.

Ana sits up, grabs a towel, and spreads it over our laps. Then she carefully serves the chips, burgers, and nuggets between us before clapping her hands. '*Bon Appétit!*'

As she chews on a burger, Ana finds the remote to the comically large TV mounted on the wall. She flicks through the channels until she finds the end of a movie. I don't recognise it, and maybe Ana doesn't either. But it's something to watch.

Ana steals more of my fries as we eat, but I don't really mind. I'm not that hungry, and the buzz of alcohol is leaving me knackered. I glance a look beside me only to find Ana sunk deep in the pillows, her eyes droopy and a single chip raised in the air as if she was a machine that's run out of steam before the chip made it to her mouth.

There are empty burger boxes scattered around us. Plucking them from the bed, I toss them into the paper takeaway bag and throw it to the floor.

'I should have taken my makeup off,' she mutters. 'But I'm too tired.'

'You have stuff in your bag?' I ask.

Ana nods. 'I have wipes in my makeup bag in the bathroom.'

Swinging my legs off the bed, I wander into the bathroom and find the small pack of wipes at the bottom of Ana's makeup bag. I piss, change into my boxers and wipe the day off my face.

'Right,' I say, jumping back into bed. The room smells like takeaway and perfume. 'Let me.'

Ana laughs as I drag the makeup wipe down one half of her face. Her dark eyeshadow smears down her cheek, her nude lipstick running onto her chin. She laughs and tries to grab at the wipe.

'No,' I say. 'Let me.'

Carefully, I run the makeup wipe over her face again. This time, the eyeshadow budges, and her mascara melts away. I rub it over the swell of her bottom lip, the curve of her jaw, the shape of her cheekbone. Turning the makeup wipe over, I work on the other side of her face until it's clean.

'That was nice,' Ana says, tiredness edging her voice. 'Unexpected. Fun.'

'Fun?'

'Yeah,' she replies, edging closer. 'I don't remember the last time I've had that much fun.'

'Not the night we went axe-throwing?'

She snorts into her pillow. 'That *was* fun.'

A curl falls over Ana's face. I reach forward and push it back, tucking it behind her ear. 'You need to have more fun.'

'I do,' she agrees.

Then she pushes forward and kisses me. It's electric. I kiss her back. She tastes like champagne and burgers and it's incredible. Her mouth opens and she coaxes me in. After everything, after weeks of back-and-forth, I'm so hungry for her. We may be drunk, but she's not a drunk kisser, and—

'I can't.' I pull away, pushing Ana across the mattress. 'We're drunk.'

Ana's brow furrows; a wrinkle appearing above the bridge of her nose. 'What?'

'We've had a lot to drink,' I say. 'I want to, but not now.'

Ana's tongue darts out to lick her lips. She nods. 'No, you're right. We've had a big night.'

'But I want a raincheck on my kiss.'

She laughs as she rolls onto her back. 'Should I write you out a voucher?'

'That would be nice, actually.' I nudge her and those dark eyes flick to mine. 'I like you a lot, Ana.'

She huffs out a little laugh like she doesn't take me seriously, but I see genuine doubt in her eyes.

'I do,' I confirm. 'Really like you.'

For my heartfelt confession, I'm rewarded with a mouth full of cotton as Ana reaches behind her to grab a spare pillow and shove it in my face.

'Go to sleep.'

Wedging the pillow underneath me, I roll onto my stomach. 'Just for the record,' I mutter. 'You kissed me.'

'Just go to sleep,' Ana replies as she and then turns the light out.

CHAPTER FIFTEEN

The alarm blares and I jolt awake. Bright light streams through the open window. Guess we didn't shut the curtains last night.

Jordan snorts awake, his arms wrapped around his pillow. His hair is a mess of curls, frizzy from sleep. Groaning, he rolls onto his back and runs a hand down his face.

'Hey.' His voice is rough. 'God, my head hurts.'

'I have some aspirin in my handbag.' As I get up to find my bag, the room spins and I brace myself on the edge of the mattress, sucking in long, deep breaths. How much did I have to drink last night? Far too much, clearly. I get up and find my bag near the minibar.

'Here.' I toss the packet onto the bed. 'I'm going to have a shower. We have to leave in thirty minutes to get to your sister's.'

Jordan swallows the painkillers dry. 'You know, we'll halve our time if we shower together.'

I scoff as I grab my fresh clothes. 'Nice try.'

Closing the door to the bathroom, I hang the towel on the hook and do my best to ignore my reflection; I can't help but catch the smudge of black around my eyes—eyeliner Jordan missed with the makeup wipe—and the sallowness of my skin. When I was younger, my skin wouldn't show my hangover. I'd be fresh-faced and glowing after a quick shower. Now, I have a few drinks or stay up past midnight and my skin turns pallid and dull. Thank God for concealer.

I shower quickly, run a comb through my hair, clip it up and get dressed. 'All yours,' I say to Jordan as I emerge in a cloud of steam. To my surprise, he's cleaned up the apartment and packed his things, ready for a quick checkout.

He kisses my bare shoulder as he passes, closing the bathroom door behind him. The kiss from last night still hangs between us; the words we'd whispered in the quiet of the early morning. I should say something, but what? In the stark light of the morning, everything looks different. *We* look different.

As Jordan showers, I put on a quick face of makeup and then grab my phone from its charging station. I take a snapshot of the award and send Erin the photo; she'd still be asleep, but it's something nice to wake-up to, I suppose.

Jordan buttons up his shirt as he steps out of the bathroom, and the scent lemongrass follows him. To my surprise, he's wearing a crisp white button-down t-shirt that hugs his chest and arms, and tan chinos and boat shoes. Even his hair, which is usually curly and wild, is slicked back and gelled into perfect waves.

'What in the world are you wearing?' I say, not trying to hide my shock.

'This is my alter ego,' Jordan replies, tossing his

toiletry bag back into his satchel. 'Rich preppy kid from inner Sydney. Don't worry. I'll put my hoodie on when we go to the airport.'

We zip up our suitcases and, after double-checking we've left nothing in the room, walk down to the lifts.

'I feel like I'm underdressed compared to you,' I say.

'Whatever you say, Miss Gucci slippers.' He looks down at the Princetown leather slippers on my feet and raises an eyebrow. 'Don't think I didn't notice them.'

'Excuse me, these were a gift from a client. I would never spend this amount of money on a pair of shoes.' Secretly, I'd had my eye on a pair for years before they'd been gifted and had been squirrelling away money to buy a pair for Christmas.

As we take a taxi to Megan's home, my phone vibrates in my handbag. It's Erin.

We are officially lice-free, but you'll need to re-dose in a week's time. Look forward to that!

She sends through a photo of Poppy's hair, now dry and lice free.

Thank you. And sorry again! Tell Pops I'll be home soon.

I turn off my phone and toss it back into my bag. Beside me, Jordan lets out a long sigh and runs his hands down his pant legs. He's nervous. Before I think better of it, I reach out and squeeze his knee. Jordan turns and looks at me, clearly surprised.

'It'll be okay,' I say.

He huffs out a disbelieving laugh but overlaps his hand with mine, squeezing. 'I just can't shake the feeling I'm walking into a trap.'

'Fucking hell!' the driver shouts as his foot slams on the break. The car lurches and we both fall forward. On instinct, my hands rise in front of me to brace my fall of the driver's seat. The car grinds to a stop, but we come dangerously close to the rear of a Porsche.

'Sorry about that,' the driver mutters. Traffic starts moving again and we inch slowly forward. Jordan looks at me, and we both try to stifle our laughter.

We cross the Sydney Harbour Bridge, a great novelty. Boats are stark white dots scattered across the flat, grey water. As we come off the bridge, the driver turns left, and we pass the Royal Botanic Gardens; a lush parkland lined with palm trees sprouting through the foliage like fingers.

'What suburb does your sister live in?' I ask, realising Jordan's put the address into the app.

'Bellevue Hill,' he replies. 'We're almost there.'

If you'd told me twelve months ago, I'd be meeting the Premier of New South Wales for breakfast, I would have laughed. But as we make our way into the inner eastern suburbs, and the streets become noticeably quieter, less compacted, the reality I'd always pushed away smacks me in the face: that people like Jordan, with their old money and closed communities, create the policies and laws that shape life for the rest of society, and that has never changed. Money stays in these buildings. In these seats of power. And it rarely shifts.

We come to a stop in front of a Spanish revival home. It's stone, painted white with rusted red accents. A rendered brick fence topped with black iron spikes surrounds the estate and as we step up to the large, monitored gate, I look up to see no less than three security cameras trained on us.

Jordan presses the intercom.

'It's me.'

A stern, male voice replies, 'That's not an identification.'

'Tate,' Jordan replies too-warmly. 'Nice to hear from you again.'

'Identify yourself.'

'It's Jordan Templeton,' he replies into the speaker. A moment passes and then the gate buzzes open. Jordan leans down to the intercom again. 'Thank you, Tate.'

'Get your ass inside,' Tate replies. 'They croissants are getting cold.'

Jordan laughs and takes my hand, leading me through the front gate and to a small, pebbled court-yard. I can hear people talking in the backyard. Jasmine hangs off the beams of a large pergola, the fragrance almost overwhelming as we walk through it and open a side gate.

'Hey everyone,' Jordan calls as we round the side. There's a subtle hint of nervousness in his voice, and just as I notice it, he lets go of my hand as we step onto the back patio. Four people are sitting around a table loaded with food. Megan is one of them: she wears a light gingham dress with her short blonde hair tied back into a tiny ponytail, emphasising her undercut. There's a cuff on the top of her ear, and a large flower tattoo covers her right shoulder. She's so much cooler than she is on TV, and I desperately want to be her friend.

'I didn't think you'd make it,' Megan says with a smile. 'Do you want a coffee, and maybe a painkiller on the side?'

He gives Megan a dirty look; something so quin-tessential among siblings. 'Everyone, this is Ana. Ana, this is Ryan, Megan's husband,' I shake hands with a burly dark-haired man with an impressive beard. 'And Julia, my niece.' Julia is one or two years older than

Poppy. She wears a black polka dot dress with bright striped stockings. I assume, like Poppy's zaniest ensembles, she's chose it herself. 'And then, well, you've met Tate. He's my sister's head of security.'

Tate wears black suit pants and a cotton t-shirt; professional and yet casual enough for breakfast. He reaches forward to shake my hand, and I can't help but notice the way his biceps flex under his shirt.

'Been slacking off the protein,' Tate says to Jordan, and he looks a little sheepish.

'Yeah, I don't remember the last time I stepped into a gym,' he replies. 'But clearly, you haven't been skipping any sessions. At the rate you're going you won't be able to wear anything but sleeveless shirts eventually.'

That makes Tate laugh.

'Coffee?' Megan says again. She stands up but Jordan waves for her to sit back down as he goes inside.

'I'll get it. I know where everything is.'

He steps through the French doors, pulled back to enjoy the crisp early morning. Inside, I can see their living room. It's covered in toys and children's books, remotes and coasters askew on the coffee table. Past the lounge area, Jordan makes coffee in a modestly sized Spanish-inspired kitchen with a large aga oven nestled into a stone inlet.

'Ana,' Megan says, pulling my attention. 'Come sit.'

She gestures to a chair beside her. The table is full of food; a deep-dish quiche with golden cheese on top, a small pile of croissants, muffins and danishes, and fresh fruit on a large ceramic platter. I wonder if this is how they eat normally, or if they've done it just for us. Jordan returns a moment later and places a flat white in front of me.

'What a talented barista you've turned out to be,' Ryan teases.

'That's why they pay me the big bucks,' Jordan responds as he sits down opposite me. 'Twenty-two dollars an hour.'

'I think it's great you got a job while at uni,' Megan replies. 'When I was getting my degree, I was a receptionist for a few days a week.'

'You were a receptionist at the premier's office,' Jordan says. I'm sure there's more to the story, more strings that were likely pulled by their father.

Megan must see it for what it is: a slight jab. She pauses, relents. 'That's true. Dad did set up the interview.'

'So how is life down in Melbourne?' Ryan changes the subject as he reaches forward to grab a slice of quiche from a platter. I take a ham and cheese croissant, but instantly regret my decision when the flaky pastry falls onto my shirt as I take a bite.

'It's good,' Jordan replies. I can't tell if it's the truth, or not. 'I play music a few times a week. Classes are good. I also tutor students, oh, and I learnt the banjo. Turns out it's not that different from the guitar.'

'No big break?' Tate asks from across the table.

Jordan gives him a tight smile. 'Working on it.'

I'd thought this was the side of the family Jordan got on with the best; yet the conversation feels heavy and loaded with barbs. It almost feels like a performance.

'He is an excellent musician, though,' I feel the need to add.

'He was always playing something growing up,' Megan says. 'Saucepans as drums, this little plastic recorder he got in a Christmas cracker one year.'

'Dad ended up breaking it accidentally,' Jordan grimaces. 'Promised to buy me a real one. Never did.'

'Well, now Julia's learning the recorder at school,' Megan says, and Julia lights up. 'Aren't you, hon?'

Julia nods but says nothing; shy with the adult company. Jordan leans in. 'What can you play?'

'Um, *Hot Cross Buns* and *Happy Birthday*, and *Scarborough Fair.*' She pauses and looks to Jordan. 'You want me to play for you?'

'Oh, no sweetie,' Megan starts.

'I'd love it,' Jordan interrupts. Julia pushes herself out of her chair to get her recorder and I stifle a laugh as Megan fixes Jordan with a dark glare.

'What?' he says, feigning innocence.

'I knew we should have invited your father,' Ryan mutters.

After breakfast at Megan's, Jordan and I catch a cab into the city to meet with the previous Minister for Housing and Development, a meeting I'd teed up last night after meeting her at the award ceremony. Jordan tells me he'll linger in a nearby coffee shop during the meeting; but when I go to find him, I see he's taken up residence on a public piano; the kind that encourages just anyone to play.

He's deep in the middle of a song, though I don't recognise it. People gather around him, mesmerised by the performance. I hang back, careful not to distract him until he's done. His fingers fly over the keys, careful and fast and beautiful in their preciseness. It's clear he has a mastery over the instrument only a few have, and when he finishes, the crowd around him bursts into applause.

His gaze meets mine, and he steps away from the piano, which is disappointing because I would have liked to watch him play another song.

'How did the meeting go?' he asks as he gets to me.

'Good. She really liked our plan and gave us a few contacts in Melbourne to follow up with.'

He checks his watch. 'Should we head to the airport?'

'Back to dreary Melbourne weather.' It's been unseasonably lovely in Sydney this weekend, and I am loath to leave the warmth.

As we arrive at the airport, I look up at the screen of flights and suppress a groan. Jordan, beside me, is less discreet.

'Fuck.'

Every flight to and from Sydney has DELAYED displayed beside it. A monster of a storm passing over Melbourne, disrupting flights. What did I say about the dreary weather?

We sit in the gate's corner, both nursing lukewarm, overpriced coffees. Jordan scrolls through his phone, his leg bouncing nervously beside mine.

'You okay?' I ask quietly. I don't need to be quiet. It's a mid-afternoon flight and the gate isn't busy.

Jordan hums and puts down his phone. 'I'm fine.' He pauses; thinks better of it. 'Just got a song on my mind, getting kinda agitated that I can't figure it out.'

'Oh,' I say. 'Well, I guess it'll come to you.'

I've never been creative, so I can't really relate to the trials of creation. Whenever I have free time, I'll watch an episode of *Grey's Anatomy* and I'll always pick up the next Liane Moriarty book, but I've never thought about the process—the creative process—around making something like that. How difficult it must be. Jordan writes lyrics into his phone, and then a series of notes underneath it.

I wonder if we should talk about last night. To be honest, I don't really know what to say. Don't really know what we are now. It was one night—one great night—with a kiss and then a morning with his family.

But even now, Jordan's knee nudges mine, a soft smile as he looks at me out of the corner of his eye. It means something to him.

We are something to each other.

Ladies and gentlemen, a woman says over the intercom. *We now welcome those boarding the delayed flight QT841 to Melbourne.*

'That's us,' Jordan says, springing from his seat. He slings his duffel bag over his shoulder, ready to board like the plane will take off without us.

The flight is quick—just over an hour—and I resolve to come up with an answer about our relationship by the time we land. But when the tires hit the tarmac, I'm no closer to figuring out if I should raise it, or if we let sleeping dogs lie.

And what would be the benefit of bringing it up? Of labelling something so quickly?

I look to Jordan, his eyes closed as he listens to music, and know I want to kiss him again. Get coffee with him in the early mornings or get a pizza with him on a Friday night.

But as the lights from the cabin hit his features; his soft skin, his five o'clock shadow, I'm reminded just how young he is. I'd wanted fun; and I'd got that. But what kind of twenty-something would be interested in dating a thirty-one-year-old woman seriously? It might be a projection, a mix of my own insecurities, but if I could go back and do my early twenties again, I wouldn't want a relationship.

I wouldn't be interested in a relationship with an older man who had a child.

So why would Jordan even consider that?

After the weekend we've had, I decide it's too much to bring up. Besides, there's a chance this whole thing might just blow over. It'll just be a fun weekend that we look back on and laugh.

It's not until we're in my Mercedes, weaving through the mid-afternoon traffic that Jordan finally brings it up.

'So, should we talk about it?' he says it so quietly I almost don't catch it over the radio.

Frankly, I don't want to talk about it. Don't want to ruin a fantastic weekend away. Don't want to face that I'm in my thirties with a kid; that I'm over the hill.

Most of all, I don't want to face that Jordan thinks the same way I do.

'Do you wanna talk about it?'

He pauses for a moment, before he says in one long breath, 'Well, technically, I'm not your client anymore, so if you want to do this, you know, we could?'

I glance at him as we stop at a red light. 'Do what?' Because I need labels. Structure. Order. I need to know what he thinks we're doing together.

He shrugs. 'Have fun. Maybe see where it leads?'

Have fun. Those two words stick to me; they're like a double-edged sword.

I choose my words carefully. 'I'm not at the same point in my life as you are.'

'I mean, that's pretty clear.' He laughs a little and

just as I think it's a jab at my age, he adds, 'We're driving in your Mercedes.'

I look at him, and it only confirms my decision. 'I don't think I can do 'fun' with you, Jordan. That period of my life is over. I want something serious.'

Jordan lets out a long sigh, his fingers drumming on the car door. His silence is answer enough.

'I don't think you want that,' I continue. 'You're not looking for that.'

'But I like you, Ana. Isn't that enough to start?'

If I was ten years younger, it would have been enough. More than enough. But as I look at Jordan, all I see is potential. Unabashed, unbridled potential. A wild horse that I don't want to tame.

'No,' I say at last. 'I don't think it is.'

CHAPTER SIXTEEN

Ana drops me at my apartment, her car coming to a smooth stop by the curb. Talia's little cream Volkswagen beetle is in the driveway. She must not have left for work yet.

Ana puts the car in park, and we just sit in silence, radio on mute, for one breath. Two.

'Thanks for coming with me on this trip,' Ana says. 'It was, well, it was fun.'

Fun. That word sticks to me. 'It was.'

It was fun. Incredibly fun. I try not to let my mind wander back to last night, but it's hard. I look at Ana and I want her. More than I've wanted someone before.

'I don't want this to end.' The words come out before I can stop them.

Ana's lips purse, and then she shakes her head. 'You don't know what you're getting into. I have a business and I work five, sometimes six days a week. I have a kid. I don't remember the last time I stayed out past midnight. A good evening for me is a glass of wine, watching *Frozen* for the three-hundredth time, and then going to bed before nine.'

I open my mouth to speak, but Ana continues.

'And that might be cute and fun for a few months, but that's my life all the time.' She hesitates. 'I like you, Jordan, but it's better we just break it off before—'

'Before it even starts?'

'Before we mess things up, and one of us gets hurt,' she corrects.

'You don't even want to try?'

Ana shakes her head. 'No.'

'Right, well.' I'm not sure what to say. Rejection isn't a stranger to me, but this hits harder, hurts worse than any rejection I've had before. I think it's because everything she's saying makes sense. I don't go out looking for anything serious, but that doesn't mean I'm going to walk away if the right opportunity comes along.

I've never liked going out much, and I'd watch *Frozen* a hundred times without complaint. I'd make coffee in the mornings, and we'd go out once a week and have a bit too much to drink. But there are no words that will convince Ana right now.

I unbuckle my seatbelt and pop the car door. 'I guess I'll see you around.'

'Yeah,' she says. 'Take care of yourself, Jordan.'

After grabbing my duffel bag from the boot of her car, I tap the top and she pulls out of the curb. It's late in the afternoon now; the sun's going down, and the storm's cleared. The sky is a violence of red and yellow and the most brilliant shade of orange I've ever seen. I stand on the side of the road for longer than I want to, but I can't go inside. Not until her car turns the corner and disappears.

For a moment there, I thought she might have stopped the car. Turned around.

I wonder if she looked back at me, if she saw me there and her mind faltered. Or if it only justified her decision. No idea.

Kicking the door open, I throw my duffel bag down the hallway. Talia's on the couch eating a bowl of cereal. Fruit loops and cornflakes swim in an enormous bowl of almond milk. *New Girl* is on the TV.

'Hey,' she says. 'You look beat. How was Sydney?'

I collapse into the couch. Talia reaches for the remote to pause the TV.

'You okay?' she asks cautiously.

I shrug. 'Will be. Guess I'm just stressed about my music.'

'I'm sure it'll come to you,' she says and then takes another mouthful of her fruit loops-cornflakes concoction. 'Don't sweat the small stuff.'

Talia's a nurse. Emergency department. Mostly night shift. To me, that's a mind-boggling job. I expect it's like living your life upside down; dinner is breakfast, weekends are meaningless, and you gotta save lives.

When I first moved in, I thought Talia's frankness was abrasive and a tad rude. Now it's refreshing. It'd be easy for her to say that I don't know what real stress is —stress over a dying patient doesn't exactly stack up against stressing over writing words to music. But she's never compared our jobs like that.

'Mind if I have a drink?' I ask, getting up to go to the fridge.

'Sure. Why wouldn't I?'

I grab a beer and twist the top off. 'Feels weird to have a beer while you're eating breakfast.'

She swallows down the last of her cereal and puts

the bowl on the side table. 'So, you wanna talk about it?' She checks her phone. 'I got ninety minutes before I gotta go to work.'

I take a sip of my beer. 'You ever consider going into psychiatry?'

'I saw you standing on the curb for like five minutes. It's not psychiatry,' Talia replies.

I can't bring myself to step into the cafe. I've dreaded coming back to work since the weekend, but I called in sick yesterday. The only thing keeping me here is my obligation to Laurie. I'm the one who fucked up. I'm the one who messed with the regulars when she explic-itly warned me not to; the guy who just had to shit where he ate. And for what?

There's every chance Ana will swan in with a new client and I'll be forced to wait on them. Rejection on top of humiliation.

Maybe I should just go in and quit.

I might have enough money to get by while I look for another job.

But then I remember Lavender Gardens; the place I play for Ana's mother. I love playing there, seeing the joy it brings to the folks. I don't want to give that up. But inevitably we'll run into each other, either at the cafe or the retirement home or on the street. There's no escaping her. No escaping us.

I'm about to push the door and head in when a woman's voice calls, 'Jordan?'

Fear shoots up my spine. I turn. It's Erin. She's at the end of the block, her long dark hair curled around her shoulders. Her cheeks are almost always flushed red; and this bitter morning is no exception.

'Just starting your shift?' she asks as she approaches me.

'Yeah,' I reply. 'How's the, um...,' I motion to her hair.

'Oh!' she laughs and her cheeks go redder. 'It's fine now, thanks. The worst thing is that I know they're gone, but I still feel them in there.'

I suppress the shiver that runs up my spine and open the door to the cafe. The smell of roasting coffee hits me, feels like home. Laurie smiles at us from the coffee machine, the wand squealing as she froths at the milk. For a Thursday morning, it's pretty busy. Four elderly women knit while having coffee, a woman is working on her laptop and a tired-looking man and his toddler-aged son hang by the counter as Laurie makes their order.

I grab my apron from the back and then scan in. 'You on coffee run duty today?' I ask Erin.

She must know what happened between Ana and I, but it's kinda depressing to know Ana's avoiding me as much as I'm avoiding her.

'Yeah,' she replies. 'I'll grab two flat whites and a mocha.' She slides three reusable cups across the counter.

'Mocha in the-,'

'In the Elsa cup,' I interrupt. 'Of course, this one is Ana's.'

'The kid loves *Frozen*.'

'How many times have you watched it?' I ask.

Erin rolls her eyes as she taps her credit card on the terminal. 'I couldn't tell you. But I could recite the movie, I reckon.'

Laurie turns to me, pulling her apron over her head. 'Do you mind making this order? I've been absolutely busting to go to the loo for the last twenty minutes.'

'No worries,' I reply and line Erin's cups underneath the coffee machine. Making coffee is like a meditation, a quiet series of movements that are done just so. First, the perfect amount of beans is ground to prevent wastage, then the right pressure moves through the grounds to create the shot. The milk is frothed at a precise angle. Slightly off and it will burn, scream, and curdle.

'She's been alone a long time.'

I look up to see Erin watching me. 'Sorry?'

'Her last serious boyfriend got her pregnant and ran off.'

'Oh,' I reply because I'm not sure what to say. I look around the cafe to see if anyone's listening, but they're not.

Erin continues, 'We practically raised Poppy together. Ana hasn't really dated since and she definitely hasn't introduced anyone to Poppy.'

Technically, she didn't introduce me to Poppy—it was more of a happy coincidence at her mother's nursing home.

'I know what she's like,' she continues. 'If you're serious about her, then you need to show it.'

That's easier said than done. I slide Erin's coffees across the bar. 'She's made it clear she doesn't want me, Erin. It's better if we left it.'

'I know you make her happy,' she says. 'Sometimes, she's a self-righteous pain in the ass. If you like her, you need to show her you're serious. Turn up. Put in the effort. Show her.'

She takes the coffees and stacks them in her carrying tray. 'See you, Jordan.'

I give her a tight smile as wipe down the benchtop with a tea towel. 'See you.'

Laurie, on her way back from her bathroom break, meets Erin at the front door and opens it as she leaves. They talk for a moment, but whatever they say, I can't hear. Instead, I focus on clearing a table of dirty dishes and checking on the woman working on her laptop. She orders another espresso, and I promise to get back to her as soon as I take the dishes to the kitchen.

'I'll do it,' Laurie says as she steps down into the café. I nod my thanks as I start loading the dishes into our dishwasher.

Just when I think I'm out of the woods, Laurie appears by the kitchen door.

'What did I say about fucking with the regulars?' she asks.

I straighten up. I'm well over six-foot, and broader than I have any right to be, but I can't help but cower at her tone. 'Not to.'

Laurie raises a brow. 'And what did you do?'

'Fucked with the regular.'

She shakes her head, but there's a whisper of a smile on her lips. 'I knew it. You know, you're lucky Erin's covering for you. Ana Woods brings a lot of business to this cafe.'

It occurs to me this might not be the only morning Erin's done the coffee run this week. Of course, Laurie was going to notice Ana's disappearance and put two-and-two together.

'Anyway,' she continues. 'I'm sorry it didn't work out.' There's real empathy in her tone. 'You'd be good to each other.'

The fact that she thinks we'd be good together is surprising to me. We're so fundamentally different but I know that spark—that feeling you get when you connect with someone—can be so luminous it's noticed by everyone around you. I think about how Laurie is with Seojun, how her face brightens, and her steps are lighter, and how I'd thought they'd be good together.

I want them to give it a shot.

A chance.

'Thanks,' I mutter. 'Me too.'

CHAPTER SEVENTEEN

I look up as Erin places a coffee cup on my desk. 'You just had to break that kid's heart, didn't you?'

Abandoning the email I was writing, I grab the reusable Elsa cup and take a long sip. To my dismay, Erin plops herself in the seat opposite me. Clearly, we're talking about this.

'I'm sure he's fine, Erin.'

She scoffs. 'You didn't see him just now. Sulking around. Shirt barely ironed.'

'He's a man in his twenties; that's their natural state.'

'Oh, cut the shit,' she replies. Her tone startles me. Erin never raises her voice. 'It got real, and you got scared.'

'I'm not scared.'

Erin looks pointedly at my coffee cup. 'So that's not why you've asked me to grab coffee for the last few days?'

Guilt hits me harder than I expect it to. Inviting Jordan to Sydney was a mistake. Kissing him was a mistake. Letting myself be vulnerable around him was a fucking mistake. I should have known better. My heart can't be trusted; it is a gentle, wild thing. It believes and loves and trusts to easily and now it's gone and fallen for something it can't have.

'It would just hurt us both. He doesn't want something serious. It'd just be fun.'

She looks at me like I've grown a second head. 'What's so wrong about that? Have fun. Go dancing. Go drinking. Shag him. Have *fun*.'

'It's not that simple. I want something serious. Someone serious.'

'You're making it complicated,' Erin rebuffs. 'You can't just expect someone to commit to you on the first date, Ana. Sometimes you just have to have a bit of fun to see where it leads.'

'I can't subject Poppy to that.'

It feels like this argument is getting out of control fast.

Erin rolls her eyes. 'You always have an excuse, you know that?'

'I don't,' I reply but there's no power in it. Maybe I do always have an excuse. Maybe I'm too inflexible, too stuck to my schedule, too caught up in my own world, but that's a can of worms I don't want to open right now.

'I just think you're cutting him off because you're scared,' she says at last and it's like she's held a mirror up, and I'm seeing the worst version of myself. In a single sentence, she's boiled down the crux of my insecurities and thrown them at my face.

I don't know what to do.

I don't know what to say.

So, like the adult I am, I take a long sip of my coffee and turn pointedly back to the computer.

Erin scoffs. 'What? Are you ignoring me now?'

'Bye Erin,' I say to the computer. She huffs and gets up, grabbing her coffee cup.

'You're such a child,' she mutters as she walks out of the office. 'Next time go get your own coffee!' she calls down the hall.

'I will,' I mutter, but it's a half-hearted comeback. Truth is, I know I've screwed up. I'm the one who brought Jordan here, who wanted to help him. Now I've probably alienated him from this place; made him nervous about going to work and burnt a bridge with Laurie.

A right mess I've made of everything.

All because I couldn't face the idea that Jordan was being truthful. Hiding behind my need for stability so I wouldn't get hurt. Routine and stability keep people safe. Secure. I've worked so long for security in my life, in my career, that it was natural I grew protective of it.

And then came Jordan with his axe-throwing nights and his hidden beach coves, his beautiful eyes and curly swoop of hair. The stupid covers he plays for Mum at Lavender Gardens and how she told me he's shown up every other Saturday for the past few months. Stupid.

I push Jordan from my mind and turn back to the contract on my desk: a multi-million-dollar contract for a set of derelict townhouses in the southern suburbs of Melbourne, and a loan application to match.

Work will make me feel better, I resolve. It'll keep my mind off the royal mess I've made of my life.

Our solicitor, Tania, rings me at half-past eleven. Though I have a Bachelor of Law, I practised for barely a year before I fell pregnant. Besides, it's always good to have a second set of eyes. Especially when figures run into seven-digits.

'There's a lot of work that needs to be done,' Tania says. 'It's a big undertaking.'

I know she's talking about the blood, sweat, and tears required to transform the old Holloway town-house block into actual living apartments. 'Still, the owner doesn't have any other prospective buyers who don't want to demolish.'

'Incredible,' I reply. 'Someone who values history over money.'

Tania hums in agreement. 'Seems you both came along at the right time.'

Erin was the lead on finding the Holloway Houses and as I hang up the call, I regret fighting with her this morning. For how childish I'd been.

If our plan works, it'll cost a mint to get the houses to habitable standard, but it'll be cheaper than trying to outbid investors for empty blocks and then build ourselves. If we can secure Holloway, we'll buy ourselves a shorter turn around. Better for our pocket, and better for our clients.

After the call, I send the contract back to the solicitor, copying Erin into the email. She doesn't reply. Probably too busy throwing darts on a cut-out of my face in her office.

A knock on the door pulls me away from my work. Olivia, the receptionist, stands holding a cup of coffee.

'This is for you,' she says and crosses the floor to hand it to me. She probably heard our fight earlier. I can't help but feel embarrassed about that. As grown as we are, sometimes we still fight like sisters.

'You didn't have to do that,' I say, but take the coffee.

Just as I realise there's a sticky-note attached to the cup, Olivia says, 'I didn't. Jordan did.'

'Oh.' I don't really know what to say. The post-it note clings to the rigid edges of the paper cup and the words *I'm serious* are scrawled onto the yellow paper.

I look up at Olivia. 'Well, um, thank you for delivering this.'

'You're welcome,' she replies, embarrassment clear in her tone. She leaves my office in a hurry.

I take a sip of the coffee.

It's good.

Damn him.

It's been a hell of a week. As I pick Poppy up from preschool, I feel like I can finally take a breath. For once, I'm not late to the school gate. I don't remember a time I actually sat in the line of cars in the pickup lane. Normally, I'm so late I pick up my daughter like I'm going through the McDonald's drive thru. Occasionally, she's been one of the last kids waiting with her preschool teacher, and I loathe the mix of understanding and sympathy in their eyes.

Busy single mum, those eyes say, I get it.

Those eyes aren't so sympathetic today. As Poppy climbs into the back seat, her teacher thrusts a leaflet through the passenger door. Printed on the leaflet with big bold black letters is: *NITS OUTBREAK—please check your child's hair as soon as possible! DO NOT bring your child to school if they have nits.*

'I went to school when I had nits,' Poppy says once I've, thankfully, wound the window up.

'I know, baby, but that's because we didn't know.'

No doubt this letter is because of Poppy. She's patient zero. 'But we've already treated them, so hopefully they don't come back. But you need to tell me if you feel itchy again.'

'Sure,' she says nonchalantly. I know I'll be checking her hair every night over the next few weeks.

When we get home, Mouse lets know she's starving with a high-pitched cry, so I dump my handbag on the lounge and grab her bowl and kibble. As I arrange everything, I go over the evening plan in my head: feed the cat, order a pizza, feed the kid, feed myself, get the kid to bed and then find something mind-numbing to watch on TV.

It all goes to plan until the kid has a tantrum because there's an olive on her slice of pizza, then the cat throws up on the rug. Finally, Greg Pryor emails me at ten-thirty-two on a Friday to top off a supremely shitty day.

Your tenant has defaulted on rent. She's out in ten days unless she pays.

Asshole. I turn off the light, exhausted. I barely got a comb through Poppy's hair, let alone a chance to wrangle her into the bath before bed. She ate half her tea, and I think I had more wine than food just trying to get through the night. My head is spinning, and I feel a kind of tiredness that makes my bones ache.

The morning comes too soon. Poppy's awake on the wrong side of 6 am, and the cat is taking up half the bed. As I swing my legs over the side of the mattress, my muscles groan with protest.

I make my way into the kitchen and Poppy and the cat follow me like a sleep-deprived version of the party train. The city is still dark; lights of the skyscrapers twinkling like stars. I turn on the coffee and while I wait for it to warm up; I make Poppy a Milo.

'Can we take Nan some flowers today?' Poppy asks from the counter.

'Na-,' I stop myself. Shit. It's Saturday. With the Sydney trip last weekend, I've completely forgotten about our visit to see Mum at Lavender Gardens.

'Definitely,' I correct myself. 'We'll have to see what's in season at the florist.'

Turns out there's an early harvest of tulips; the florist is awash with them. We buy a small bouquet of yellow tulips, and I get Mum a coffee at a local cafe.

She's happy to see us as we walk through the door. Her eyes light up, so I know she's recognised us. With dementia, every day is a battle. The day she doesn't recognise us will kill me. Erin and I know it's coming; we can only stave off Mum's dementia for so long. I still don't know how I'm going to explain it to Poppy. I only hope she'll be a little older when it happens.

Today, she's sitting by the window, bathed in a ray of sunlight with yet another crochet blanket project draped over her legs. Poppy and I take a moment to disinfect our hands before making our way across the room.

'My girls,' she smiles.

'Hey Mum,' I say as I hand her the coffee. 'We got this for you.'

She takes a sip of the coffee and sighs. 'Nothing better. Thank you.' The staff at Lavender Gardens are wonderful, but they don't make a coffee like the Italian bloke by the florist. Strong. Rounded. Mum drinks it black; no sugars. Ordering a mocha would be a travesty to her.

'And the flowers,' Poppy adds, placing the bright collection of tulips on her lap.

'Thank you, dear. They'll brighten up the room.'

One of the nurses takes the flowers from Poppy, places them in a small vase and takes them back to Mum's room.

'You didn't come through last week?' Mum says.

Guilt slams into me. 'Sorry, I thought Erin would have let you know? I was in Sydney and Erin and Poppy had nits.'

'Nits?" she echoes.

'*Vši*,' I clarify. The Czech feels strange to my tongue. By the look on my mum's face, she's not thrilled with my pronunciation.

'Ah, *vši*,' she echoes, her accent coming through. 'Awful.'

'Yes, Erin had them too.'

Mum's eyes move from mine. Something's caught her attention on the other side of the sunroom, and before I can turn to look, I hear the unmistakable strum of guitar strings. I turn to see Jordan dragging a stool across the room, his guitar slung over his shoulder. Other residents are making their way into the room; their faces lit with smiles.

Mum takes my hand, squeezes. 'He comes all the time.'

'Does he?' I ask. I turn my chair around to sit beside Mum and pull Poppy into my lap. Jordan busies himself by setting up his water bottle and fiddling with the microphone. It's certainly an improved set-up from the first time I saw him perform.

'We ask him to learn songs and he does,' she says. 'He's good fun.'

'He is,' I admit.

Jordan's eyes sweep over the audience as he prepares to sing; but he doesn't look at me. I'm sure he's noticed me, but we're so deep into the game of avoidance that we'll continue to orbit around each other like planets; with inner south Melbourne our sun.

Jordan leans into the microphone. 'Thanks for having me back, folks. This one goes out to Emily.'

A woman, presumably Emily, claps and cheers from her wheelchair as Jordan launches into a cover of Sweet Caroline by Neil Diamond. I'm surprised he knows the residents by name but it's clear he's got a rapport with them because by the end of the song, the room's singing along. I never knew he was such a performer. I know people say they become someone different on stage, but this persona just feels like another layer of Jordan. He's charismatic, playful and a little flirty and the residents lap it up.

He's playing at my mum's retirement village; in a room of maybe fifty people, but he acts like he's in an arena.

As he winds down from Neil Diamond, he takes a long sip of water and then starts plucking the deep chords of Elvis's *Suspicious Minds*.

'Did you request anything?' I ask Mum.

Poppy pipes up with what is *definitely* not her inside voice: 'I want the Elsa song!'

Mortifyingly, that gets Jordan's attention. His eyes slide over to our side of the room and the corners of his mouth curl into a smile.

'Ladies and gentlemen, the lady has spoken,' he says into the microphone. He turns back to his guitar and his fingers strum out a delicate melody. An all-too-familiar melody. I had no idea he'd learnt to sing Let It

Go, but his acoustic version is beautiful. Haunting, even.

Poppy claps as Jordan finishes playing, pulling his guitar off his shoulder.

'Five-minute break, everyone,' he says into the microphone.

To my surprise, he walks over to us, a bashful smile on his face. How quickly he returns to the Jordan I know after stepping off the stage. Warmth simmers in his gaze.

'I didn't think you'd be here,' he says. 'But I'm glad you are.'

'I didn't think you'd learn *Let It Go*,' I parrot. 'But I'm glad you did.'

A huff of a laugh escapes his lips as he looks to Poppy. 'You like it, Pops?'

She nods shyly, moving her weight from foot-to-foot. 'Could you teach me how to play it?'

Jordan looks at me for approval in that way all adults do when posed big questions by children. I nod. 'I sure can,' he tells her. 'But the guitar is too big for you right now, but maybe I can teach you on the piano?'

Poppy's eyes light up with excitement. Beside me, my mother laughs at the spectacle. All I think is that I'll likely be buying Poppy a keyboard for Christmas.

'I gotta get back,' Jordan says after a minute. He nods back to the crowd. 'My fans are waiting.'

'Please, don't let us keep you,' I say and pull Poppy back onto my lap.

'You gonna stick around for morning tea?' he asks.

I nod. 'Yeah, we'll stay.'

'Cool.'

With that, he jumps back onto his barstool and

slings his guitar over his shoulder. The window's open, and the smell of incoming rain washes through the stuffy sunroom. I daydream of an afternoon spent on the couch with a good book and a warm drink.

Jordan plays a handful of songs; upbeat and fun and designed to encourage the residents to groove, however mobile they may be. Mum claps along beside me. Another man taps along to the beat with his walking stick. The nurses hang towards the back of the room, just observing. It must bring them some relief, I realise. Some time to catch up on paperwork; to make a coffee.

Jordan finishes his set and receives a rapturous applause from the crowd. Someone whistles from the back of the room. Jordan bows once, twice, and then leans into the microphone. 'You're a great crowd! I'll be back next Saturday!'

More applause. The nurse takes the microphone with a kind smile and announces morning tea is served in the main dining room. As the residents move out, Jordan bounds over to us, clearly energised by the high of performance.

'Let's go get some cucumber sandwiches,' he says, completely serious. We walk into the main hall and find a seat. A large platter of sandwiches, fresh fruit and biscuits is set up on each table. The nurses serve hot drinks to the non-mobile residents, but the rest of us line up in front of an old tea and coffee station.

After avoiding each other all week, Jordan and I stand in line to use the coffee machine. Neither of us speaks. The silence is uncomfortable. Awkward. I desperately want to break it, but I have no idea what to say. Do I mention the post-it note?

'I'm performing next Saturday night,' he says, and

I'm so busy thinking about conversation starters that I miss it.

'Huh?'

'I wrote a piece for a prize at school. Somehow, I'm a finalist. I'm performing next Saturday night. I wanted to know if you'd come?'

'I'd love to.' The words tumble from my mouth before I can stop them. Not that I would have said no; but the betrayal of my body in Jordan's presence is an annoying recurrence lately. 'I can't believe you learnt how to play *Let It Go*.'

Jordan shrugs. 'It wasn't hard.'

'It meant a lot to her.'

He looks back at Poppy and smiles. 'I'd like to teach her how to play the piano. If that's cool with you.'

I nod. 'It's cool with me.'

'You'll be seeing a bit more of me, then,' Jordan badgers. 'No avoiding.'

I scoff. 'Excuse me, I was very busy all week.'

'You didn't respond to my note,' he says as we finally get to the coffee machine. Seems we are talking about it, then.

I grab a paper cup from the large stack. Jordan leans over, smelling like musk and sweat, and pinches it from me. Damn him.

'I am still thinking about my response,' I reply.

'Is that so?' Jordan replies as he shoves his paper cup under the coffee nozzle. 'Is it because you don't believe me?'

'N-no.' His direct questioning has caught me off guard and he knows it.

'Is it because you don't like me?'

'No.'

He leans in closer; lowers his voice. 'Is it because you think I don't like you?' he murmurs. 'Think I'll get bored?'

The shock of those words strikes through me like hot metal on an anvil. It feels like someone's struck me down; twisted and misshapen the core of me, and the sad little insecurities I keep locked there have found a way out of their cage. I almost crush the paper cup in my hand. 'I don't—,'

'That's what you think, isn't it?' Jordan murmurs. The coffee machine splutters out a latte. He takes it and just as he turns to go back to our table, he leans down. 'I won't.'

Stealing a marker, Jordan grabs my coffee cup and scrawls something on the ridged brown shell.

He hands it back to me. *I'm serious* is written awkwardly around the edge of the cup.

'For when you're ready to have some *serious* fun,' he says and then throws the marker back on the table.

I close my eyes and stab at the coffee machine. The grinder whirls to life, but I don't even know what it's making. Doesn't matter. My body's already thrumming. I feel out of control but so in tune with everything around me. Everything's so much more, so hyper realistic. The curtains sway and the dust dances, suspended in beams of light. I hear Poppy's voice over the murmur of the dining room.

Mindlessly, I make my way over. Like driving on autopilot, I take a strawberry from the plate and bite into it. Mum and Jordan are having a conversation, but I can't make out what it is. Somewhere outside, in the far distance, thunder rolls.

Fuck my life.

CHAPTER EIGHTEEN

It's almost the end of the semester. There are only two more weeks left until winter break, and the freezing wind whips the campus into a frenzy. I pull my jacket closer as I trudge towards my lecture theatre.

There's a small collection of students in the stalls as I walk in. I catch the gaze of Marco, hanging out in the back rows, and pointedly ignore him. Taking a seat, I throw down my satchel and pull out my notebook. *Introduction to Song Theory* isn't the most enlightening of subjects, but it's an easy pass if you turn up.

The lecturer drones on, and I take notes between sips of coffee. An hour later, I shoulder my satchel back on and use my phone to check when the next train is; twelve minutes.

'Jordan!'

I don't have to turn around to see who it is. Marco half-jogs to catch up to me as I make my way out of the lecture building.

I turn towards the door, pushing it open. 'I'm not interested.' Icy wind rushes in, stinging my face.

Marco follows me out onto the street. It's a fucking awful day in Melbourne and I just want to go home and turn on the heater, but he's not letting up. 'I just wanted to say I was sorry for the other week.'

I turn to him, and he sees it as an opportunity to continue. 'I was coming down off a shit high and nothing was going right. The recording session was a nightmare. It doesn't excuse it, but I'm sorry I said those things.'

'You're frustrated that I'm not your money machine anymore.'

Marco huffs, shakes his head. 'We had a lot of fun pissing away your dad's money.' His mouth forms a tight line. 'But I get you gotta break off on your own. Respect it. Money makes it easy.'

I hadn't expected him to apologise. It's refreshing.

'I know I acted like a twat,' he mutters. 'You wanna go grab a drink? Get out of the cold?'

There's an old pub a block away; classic Aussie pub-grub and as soon as I think about it, my stomach rumbles. I could smash a parmy. And I see Marco's invitation as what it is: an olive branch. Hopefully, he pays for the meal, too. 'Yeah, let's go.'

'You got any plans tonight?' Talia asks as she grabs her handbag. She's dressed in dark blue scrubs, a pocket watch clipped to her front pocket. She's wrapped her long braids into a bun, and the faint smell of floral perfume follows her.

I stretch from my place on the couch. 'Hmm, no.'

She takes her lanyard from the key bowl by the front door. 'It's a Friday night.'

'And it's tit's cold. I'm probably gonna order a pizza.'

She gives me a look that's half loathing, half jealous. 'Well, have fun.'

'You too,' I say as she wrenches open the door. Cold air floods the lounge room and I burrow under the blanket further.

Talia rolls her eyes. 'Enjoy your cocoon.'

'I will, thanks!' I call out as she closes the door behind her. It's the first Friday night I haven't spent working on music, and with the presentation tomorrow night, I'm keen to have a night off. I order a pizza—a supreme with pineapple—and grab a beer from the fridge before selecting another serial killer documentary.

My phone vibrates somewhere in the layers of blankets, and I dismantle the nest I've made to find it. An unknown number pops up on the screen. *You want a drink?*

Who is this and how did you get my number? Of course, I know who it is. I don't give out my number to just anyone.

Funny, Ana replies. *You want to or not?*

It *is* cold as balls outside, but this is Ana talking. *Where you wanna meet?*

Coco's in Prahran. Meet you there in about 30?

I check the tram schedule before texting back. *See you there.*

Turning off the documentary, I put what's left of my now-cold pizza in the fridge and jump in the shower. I steal some of Talia's caramel-scented body wash and a dollop of her face cleanser, putting the bottles in *exactly* the same position as I found them as not to arise suspicion.

Once I'm dry, I scrunch mousse in my hair and throw on a hoodie and jeans. Best to keep things casual. I'm not looking to freeze my balls off by being an overdressed dick. Grabbing my sneakers from the closet, I pull them on, brush my teeth and then find my keys. My phone pings. The tram is less than two minutes away.

I rush down the street, icy wind hitting my face, and make it to the tram stop just as it's pulling in. It's toasty on board; the heater cranked to the max. Unsurprisingly, the carriage is empty.

I ride the tram through the grey, damp suburbs of south Melbourne—past the cafe and Grace House, past *Walter's* and the axe-throwing speakeasy—until I reach the spot closest to *Coco's*. I haven't been to *Coco's* before, which is surprising because it's Bermuda-themed and pink-flamingo neon lighting floods the street. It sticks out like a sore thumb. There's a line-up at the door; a bouncer is checking the ID of three young women trying to get in. Once he's satisfied, he waves us through. He doesn't ask for my ID. Don't know if that's sexist or not.

Ana's sitting underneath an electric blue neon-sign that says 'Havana Nights', and the glow. Her hair falls in voluminous waves around her shoulders. She smiles when she sees me. The bar is busy, loud music thumping, and I push my way through a crowd of bodies at the bar. Ana stands as I greet her, wearing a black turtleneck, black pants, and black boots. I wonder if she's just finished at the office.

'Wanna drink?' she yells over the music. This isn't the kind of place I'd expected us to meet. Too loud. Too noisy. Too *much*.

'Beer's fine,' I yell back.

She nods and moves towards the bar, merging into the conglomerate of bodies. I slide onto the stool next to her. At the back of the bar, there's a large dancefloor. It's barely seven, but people are already dancing. A sash flashes in the neon lights: *bride to be*.

Ana returns a minute later with two pints, and there's a moment of silence between us while we take a long drink.

'Why did you choose this place?' I yell over the music.

Ana looks around and shrugs. 'I dunno. Seemed fun. But it is pretty loud.' She points to a door leading to a courtyard. 'You wanna go out back?'

We grab our drinks and move past the stage and to the courtyard outside. It's much quieter; the music now a steady thump that I feel run through my body; like a heartbeat or a pulse. The courtyard is popular, but we find a bench and a small table in the corner, angling our bodies towards each other to talk. Our knees bump. Our shoulders brush. I'm close enough to smell what's left of her perfume; a worn, musky, spicy smell that lingers on the fabric of her turtleneck. Fairy lights hang from the rafters, dappling spots of yellow light over us.

And then, all at once, she turns and kisses me.

I don't expect it, but it's in no way unwelcome. She's soft but demanding, and she tastes a little like beer and something else I can't quite figure out. She smiles against my lips, and it's wonderful.

We don't say anything for a long while, but our bodies move closer, and we kiss. We kiss until my jaw starts to feel sore and it's wonderful. Everything about this is wonderful. My hand rests on her knee and she curls against me, nursing her drink. In our own little corner, everyone else seems far away. The beer, well-rounded and hoppy, warms my blood; I don't feel the cold bite of the night anymore. Ana relaxes against me as she drains the last of her pint.

'Well,' Ana says. 'That was a nice drink. Suppose I'll go home now.'

I laugh and wrap my arms around her waist, pinning her to the lounge.

She turns to me, mock-surprise on her face. 'Oh, would you like to come?'

I take a second to process the question. Home. With Ana. 'Sure,' is the best thing I can muster as my synapses fizzle and short out.

I finish my drink and Ana grabs her keys. Her car is parked on a side-street a few blocks away, bathed in the yellow beams of a streetlight. The first spittle of rain stings my cheeks.

We drive back to Ana's apartment. She toes her shoes off at the front door as the familiar chime of a bell draws closer. Mouse appears from the kitchen and rushes forward. Ana closes the door behind us as Mouse rubs against our legs. I reach down and scratch her cheek, surprised by how loud she's purring.

'She remembers you,' Ana observes.

'We're buds,' I reply. I never had pets growing up. 'Snuggle buddies.'

'You want another drink?' she asks as she opens the fridge door. 'I've got beer or a bottle of wine?'

'Beer's good,' I reply. Ana places a can on the bench top as she opens a bottle of merlot. I pick up Mouse and give her a snuggle, but it's clear by the claws in my shoulder she's not into it. I put her down and she scampers over to the kitchen, where Ana feeds her. It's so domestic and nice.

'Where's Pops?' I ask.

'She stays with Erin every other Friday night,' she replies. 'I think they were going to the movies tonight.' Her eyes light up, like she's just remembered something. 'Ah, I gotta show you.'

She crosses the lounge room and beckons me down the hallway, where an electric keyboard sits in a study nook. 'I got it second-hand for Poppy. I thought if she wanted to learn, a piano is a pretty solid instrument.'

'Arguably the *most solid*,' I reply as I sit down on the bench. Some musicians are obsessed with pianos, but I liked the diversity of string instruments. Still, the good thing about electric keyboards is that nothing goes out of tune. Everything sounds *right*. The music flows out of the tiny speakers, as clear and crisp as you could hope.

Ana stands beside me and as I come to the end of the composition, she sucks in a breath. 'That was beautiful. Who wrote that?'

'I did,' I reply. 'It's supposed to be on guitar, so I'm glad it sounds pretty good on the keyboard.'

'You wrote that?' she clarifies. 'Jordan, that was amazing.'

I shrug. Praise has always sat weirdly on my shoulders; I've always wanted to shake it off. 'You'll hear the authentic version tomorrow night.'

'I can't wait.' She leans down and kisses me. It's an awkward angle, so I rise from the piano seat. My hands rise to cup her cheeks and I kiss her properly; passionately. How I've wanted to kiss her all this time.

I press my mouth to the soft, warm skin of her neck and hear her breath catch. Fingers weave through my hair. The tang of acidic perfume sits on my tongue as I nose at her turtleneck.

Ana pushes herself against me and I barely contain

the groan. A hiss of a laugh escapes her wicked lips and I bite down on her earlobe in defiance.

Her hands move to my chest, and she pushes me away. For a second, I'm taken aback. Maybe I've misread this. Gone too far. But then she pushes me again; back towards the open door of her bedroom, and as I take her hand, she grins at me, her eyes seductive and dark.

The backs of my legs meet the foot of her bed, and she grins. She goes to push me again, but I grab her forearm and spin her until she's flushed with mine and she's staring into the large full-length mirror on the other side of the room.

I wrap an arm around her waist and lower my mouth to her ear. 'Look at us,' I say. 'Look at how fucking *perfect* we are together.'

I hear her breathing hitch. Her body is like a furnace against mine. We're both wearing too many clothes.

'Tell me you want this.' My fingers flick the button of her jeans. 'That you want me.'

'Please,' she replies.

I push up the knit of her turtleneck, push it over her face and head, drag it over her arms and then throw it to some dark corner of the room. She's wearing a singlet and bra underneath, and even in the dark, I can see the faint tan lines from her bikini; a remnant of a summer recently gone.

'Why are we wearing so many clothes?' I huff as I tug off my hoodie and shirt. Ana does the same, shucking off her tight jeans and singlet until she's standing before me in her underwear, and I'm in my boxers.

As her eyes travel over me, I wish I'd gone to the

university gym a little more often this semester. I'm softer than I was; the slight definition of my abs gone. I swallow down my insecurity. It's not easy, but I refuse to let the feeling stick.

I turn Ana and we face the mirror again. 'I want you just like this, here, looking at me.'

'In front of...' she trails off, meeting my gaze in the mirror.

'I want you to watch yourself. Watch me.'

She swallows audibly.

'You can say n—'

'Yes,' she interrupts. 'I want to.'

I unclasp her bra. The black lace slides down her arms and falls to the floor.

'Watch,' I say as my mouth finds the junction of her neck. Her skin breaks out into gooseflesh as I run my hand over her stomach, feel the dimples of stretch marks against her skin; smooth my palm down her hip.

I look up through my lashes. She's watching me, her eyes dark and glassy. She gasps as I palm her breast, her nipple a hard bud against my fingertips. I kiss her throat, the delicate skin behind her earlobe, inhale the scent of her hair; citrus and earthy.

My other hand finds the band of her thong, black and simple cotton. Practical. Efficient. My fingers slip inside, and I find her wet. Suddenly, her hand flies up and she grips my forearm tightly. I stop, suddenly worried I've taken it too far.

'Is this okay?' I check in.

'Yes.' Ana swallows hard. She's looking at us in the mirror. What we're doing. How we fit together. 'It's just been a while.'

I brush a kiss to her mouth, but she turns and takes me greedily. Her hand wraps around my neck, and she takes a fistful of hair at the base of my head and *tugs*. I growl against her lips like an animal, and she smiles and pulls back. Her eyes glimmer with challenge. Wild. Incredible. Beautiful.

I turn her to me, mirror be damned, and push her onto the mattress. Grabbing her thong, I slide it down her long legs and toss it across the room. Ana grins, hair splayed out underneath her, skin shining with a light sheen of sweat.

'You got a condom?' I ask because I certainly haven't; and I regret not being more prepared.

Ana nods. 'In the dresser. Check the expiry.'

Finding the box of condoms at the back of her dresser, I fish one out and check it's expiry, but it's dated until mid-next year. We're fucking lucky she had some. I grab one and toss it to her, and she catches it in the dim light.

'Hold it a sec, would you?' I don't wait for her answer as I kiss her; her mouth, her throat, the strip of skin between her breasts and then her nipple. She writhes and giggles a little as my mouth drags against the soft skin of her belly, and my hands run down her sides.

'Ticklish?' I murmur. My mouth goes lower to her belly button and the silvery stretch marks. Her knees part and I hear her take the duvet into her hands, tighten it between her fingers. I close my eyes and kiss the top of her vulva. She moans and I revel in it, tongue curling lower to find her clit. Her hips rise a little, and I smooth my hands over her hip bones, eliciting a laugh.

'Finding this funny, are you?' I murmur.

She stifles another giggle. 'No, not at all.'

It's hard to supress my own smile as I grab her

knees and set them on my shoulders. Lowering my
mouth back to her pussy, I lick a long stripe up the
centre of her and hear her gasp. Her heels drive into
my back, the firm muscles of her thighs flex under my
palms. She's vocal in her pleasure, gasping and groaning
as I push her to the edge. When I stop, she huffs out a
wordless complaint and takes a handful of my hair. She
tugs.

'Jordan,' she warns.

I suppress a laugh and focus on her clit again. It
doesn't take much longer. Her thighs tremble as she
comes, bowing off the bed and shattering. It's a beautiful thing, but I don't pull off her body to watch.
Instead, my mouth works her harder. Pushes her
further. Her heels dig into my back, and I'm sure I'll
have two perfectly circular bruises there tomorrow.

'I'm good,' she gasps eventually, tapping at my
shoulder.

I kiss her stomach, the skin between her breasts,
her clavicle as I crawl up her body. Ana pushes my
sweaty curls from my eyes and kisses me lazily; our
mouths slow and gentle.

'I still have this,' she hums after a moment, handing
me the condom.

I flip it over with my fingers, studying it. 'Cherry-
flavoured?' I mutter.

Ana rolls her eyes and pushes me off her. 'I grabbed
whatever there was at the store,' she says as she rises to
her knees. 'And I have an implant.'

'Good to know,' I reply.

I tear open the condom wrapper and roll it on.
Ana's hand covers mine and she pumps me once, twice.
My head swims and I close my eyes, sucking in a
breath. I feel the weight of the mattress shift, and then

Ana's above me, her hands braced on my chest. I grasp her hips as she slowly lowers herself onto me, taking me slow. The feeling of her is toe-curling and as finally she settles herself on me, hips flushed with mine, the air leaves my lungs in the shape of her name.

She looks down at me and grins, I love it. Fucking *love* it. Somehow, I'd knew she'd want to take control, to have power and wield it fairly. I promise myself I'll overthrow her one day, but for now, I'm happy to let her do as she likes. She rides me fast, unrelenting in her pace and rhythm. For a second, I worry it'll be over, and I almost reach up to tell her to stop, but then she throws her head back and groans my name and it's *everything*. Her thighs tighten, bracketing my hips, and then I'm gone. I come hard, moving with her until I'm spent. Until we're both spent.

Ana laughs and falls to the side, stretching her limbs. We lie beside each other for a few seconds; putting ourselves back together piece-by-piece.

Carefully, I peel the condom off. 'You want a towel?' I ask as I walk into her ensuite. I turn on the light and it's shocking in its brightness. Too much, too soon. Whatever spell has fallen on this night feels broken now. My afterglow is retreating quickly. I wonder if Ana feels the same; worry Ana feels the same.

'Please,' she replies, fatigue edging in. 'There are fresh ones under the sink.'

Disposing of the condom, I grab a hand towel and dampen it. Ana's sunk under the sheets by the time I return.

'You gonna stay?' she asks as I hand her the towel.

I stand by the bed; not willing to get in it. It seems like such a personal space now, and I'm no longer welcome. 'You want me to?'

Her brow furrows slightly. 'Of course.' She reaches forward and pushes back the covers. 'I'm pretty sure it's illegal to leave without cuddles. Besides, it's late and raining. Stay.'

'Oh, well, if it's *illegal*,' I say as I crawl into bed beside her. 'I'd better not risk it.'

'Mm-hm,' she hums into the pillow. 'It was passed through parliament a few months ago. Harsh penalties apply.'

'Do they?' I say. We shift our bodies into a comfortable position; her with her head on my shoulder and me with my hands tracing patterns up-and-down her spine. 'What would those be?'

'They cut off your dick,' Ana deadpans. I burst out laughing at the blunt delivery.

'Don't want that, do we?'

'No,' she huffs. 'We don't.'

CHAPTER NINETEEN

'Shit,' Jordan says. I'm jostled awake by the weight of his body leaving the bed. Blinking, I check the time on my phone. It's just after eight-thirty.

'What's wrong?' I ask, my voice croaky from sleep. Jordan buckles up his jeans and starts looking around the room for his hoodie.

'I got a rehearsal on at eleven. I completely forgot,' he replies as he scoops up his hoodie and pulls it over his head. 'Gotta swing by home and get my guitar.'

He leans down and kisses my forehead. 'Had a great time last night. I'll see you at the performance tonight?'

My head's swimming: this is all too quick. Too much. 'Um, yeah,' I manage out. 'Seven, right?'

'Yeah,' he says. He picks up my discarded thong, and it dangles on the end of his finger. He pulls back the elastic and aims it at me.

'Don't!' I cry in mock-terror, hiding under the covers. I hear it hit the duvet cover with a dull smack, and then the blankets are pulled away from my body. I fight against it, gripping them tightly, as Jordan lays his weight over my body, pinning me against the mattress.

I yield, pushing down the blankets, red-face and panting from laughing. Jordan smiles and pushes the hair from my face; kisses my nose.

'See you tonight,' he says.

'See you tonight,' I confirm. The words are hard to get out. It feels like my heart's in my throat.

Jordan gets up and leaves and I stay in bed until I hear the front door close behind him. Then, with a huff, I haul myself into the shower. I feel gross, and hot, and sore and incredible, and the warm water is like a balm.

After showering, I dress, turn the coffee machine on, and feed the cat. Outside, rain patters on the window. Another miserable day. I think of Jordan catching public transport and regret that I didn't think about ordering him a ride home.

Once my coffee's brewed, I curl up on the lounge and, at a loss with what to do, settle on a documentary while my hair dries in the curlers. The coffee does little to push away the dregs of sleep, and just the thought of sleep lulls me towards it. Before I know it, I'm propped up, napping in my armchair.

The sound of the doorbell jerks me awake. Erin opens the door a moment later and Poppy rushes towards me.

'Hey baby,' I say, hugging her. There's no mistaking the tiredness in my voice.

'You didn't lock your door?' Erin says as she dumps Poppy's backpack on the lounge.

I wave her off. 'I was up late last night. Must have forgotten.'

Poppy disappears into her bedroom, and Erin makes herself a coffee in the kitchen. I follow her, still groggy from the nap. It must be close to lunchtime. 'What did you two get up to?'

'We went to the movies. Got a burger. She crashed at about nine,' she replies as the coffee machine whirls to life. 'You?'

'Oh, you know,' I shrug. 'Emails. The usual.'

'You didn't go out?'

Briefly, I wonder if she can smell the deceit. If it wafts off me in waves of lies. Maybe they saw me out. They could have gone to the cinema in the Jam Factory; only a few blocks away. I'd never asked them where they were going or what they were seeing. 'No,' I shake my head. 'Too cold.'

I don't want to tell her about Jordan yet. It's not that I don't think she'd be happy for me, but whatever this is between us feels like a small delicate thing. Like a hatchling in the nest. I'll tell her soon when it's grown bigger. Stronger.

I rummage through my fridge and take out things to make sandwiches, cold meats and vegetables and jars of half-eaten chutney.

'What time do we have to be at the performance tonight?' Erin asks.

I check my smart watch. 'Six-thirty.'

She takes a sandwich triangle from the small pile and I smack the top of her hand with the flat of the knife. She chuckles and retreats with her prize. In the hallway, I hear Poppy playing the piano, punching out random notes.

'Jordan's giving her lessons,' I reply to Erin's raised brow.

'Jordan is?' she parrots. 'Interesting.'

I ignore her tone and call Poppy back for lunch. Afterwards, as the rain pours outside, we all settle in to watch a movie. Erin makes popcorn and the sticky-buttery smell lingers in the kitchen for hours.

'Why are we going out?' Poppy ask as we wait for the car to arrive downstairs. Rain falls from the building's overflowing gutters, smacking on the pavement. I hold Poppy close to me as the wind blows, shielding her with the sides of my jacket.

'My thoughts exactly,' Erin mutters beside me. I nudge her with my elbow.

'We're going to see our friend Jordan perform,' I answer.

'Friend,' Erin says. I nudge her again, but she only laughs.

The car arrives and we bundle in. Since it's such a horrid night, it's a short drive into the city and we arrive at the concert hall early. The doors are still closed, but Erin finds a dumpling place a few blocks away, and we decide to get a drink and a bite to eat. I don't remember when we've all had a night out like this; it's usually either me and Poppy or Erin takes Poppy to give me a break. Though we work together, I've missed hanging out with my sister.

The South Melbourne School of Arts Composition Prize is, it seems, a very big deal. The doors are open now, and the foyer is packed. We flash our tickets to the attendant, and he hands me a program.

'Jordan's playing second-to-last,' I say as we find a place to stand. I gaze around the room and can't help but catch a few eyes. Everyone is well-dressed and they're looking at our group with a mix of disdain and confusion. I glance down at Poppy in her pink jumper and pink tutu and pink gum boots and wonder if I should have brought her. There aren't any other kids, and I can't blame them. No kid thinks a classical music recital constitutes a fun night out.

I'm not the only one to notice the stares, it seems, as Erin whispers, 'Did Jordan say it was formal attire?'

'He didn't mention it,' I reply. It's the truth. He didn't mention any kind of dress code and Erin and I have gone with the usually reliable semi-formal. But neither of us can deny we don't fit in. Several women are in floor length gowns and all the men wear three-piece suits. Erin tries to pull down the knee-skimming hem of her black knitted dress, but it doesn't budge.

'You think he'll win?' Erin asks.

I think back to last night, when he'd played me his original piece on Poppy's second-hand piano. He'd said it hadn't sounded right, but I thought it was the most beautiful thing I'd ever heard. 'I hope so.'

Erin buys two glasses of wine from the bar as we enter the hall. It's beautiful. Large red curtains drape from the ceiling to frame the stage. We find our seats and Poppy wiggles on her booster, craning her neck to see over the head of the man in front of her. I hear someone behind me tut and I wonder if it's directed at us.

The lights dim. The crowd goes silent, and a man wearing a suit-and-tie approaches the microphone.

'Welcome ladies and gentlemen to the thirty-fifth annual South Melbourne School of Arts Composition Prize. I'm Professor Lucas Wright, the Dean of the School of Music and Composition. We're thrilled to present to you tonight ten of the school's finest composers; each of them shortlisted for the prize.'

He drones on a little about the history of the prize

and then welcomes the first performer to the stage. Stage crew wheel a large harp out from behind the dark curtains and a petite woman with a short black crop of hair approaches the crowd, bows, and then sits down to play. She finishes, and the crowd applauds stiffly.

Three more people play in close succession. I follow the names and titles of their pieces on the program. Two of them play on piano and one plays on the violin. The fourth person appears on the stage with a saxophone around his neck and plays an incredible piece. By the time he finishes, he's red in the face and sweat covers his forehead.

An intermission is called, despite it only being twenty minutes since we sat down, and the crowd files out into the foyer.

Poppy runs to the loo as I purchase the next round of wine, sandwiched by people dressed in their gowns and suits. I return to Erin and Poppy just as we're called to re-take our seats, and we shuffle back into the hall.

The next two performers play a piano and a guitar respectfully, and their pieces are lovely: beautiful in their own unique ways. If Jordan was with me, he'd have an opinion. I'm sure the surrounding people do, too. But I can't hear the faults in the music, can't discern if something is critically wonderful or awful, and I suppose that's a beautiful thing too.

The eighth performer wraps up their cello piece with a flair, striking the strings with a beautiful upward stroke. I clap and lean down to Poppy, 'Jordan's next.'

Her eyes light up and I'm grateful because she'd been fidgeting through the cello. As suspected, a classical music concert is not high on what a four-year-old categorises as a fun night out.

A stagehand brings out a stool and adjusts the microphone, and Jordan walks on stage.

'Whoo!' Erin yell-whispers as he takes a seat, her volume only high enough to scandalise the few seats around us. Save for her, the concert hall is dead quiet; and I will my daughter not to yell out that she knows the man on stage.

Jordan's fingers find their place on the guitar, and after a breath, he plays. Music flows from him and vibrates throughout the hall. As he moves through the piece, I ruminate on how he'd looked last night hunched over Poppy's keyboard, and how special the piece had sounded.

I don't think it sounds bad on the guitar. It's beautiful. This performance is for the audience, and that's fine. But it's not my version. It's not the quiet performance Jordan gave me.

He finishes his piece, rises, and bows to the audience. We clap and he moves off stage robotically. I wonder how he feels right now; if his heart is thumping or if he's calm and happy it's over. Does he think he's done well, or is he disappointed in himself?

The last performer is a flutist, and he plays a gentle, playful piece that mesmerises Poppy and earns him a tremendous applause from the audience. He bows, dark hair falling over his face, and exits stage left. The lights turn back on, and I blink through the sudden change. It always feels like you've been transported back to reality when that happens; it's the strangest feeling. One moment you're reeling after watching the performance of your life, and then poof! You're back in your normal, everyday life having just spent a hour and a half in a darkened room with complete strangers.

The Dean emerges again and steps up to the microphone. Behind him, A stagehand wheels out a table of awards.

'I'm sure you all agree that was an excellent evening of performances,' he booms into the microphone. I wish someone would tell him to step back. 'And now, to announce the winners. This prize has launched the career of musical theatre names, classical music and recording artists. The potential of excellent composition is endless, and we have seen quality craft tonight.

'And now, to the awards. Highly commended goes to Holly Trang with her piece, *Streetlights*.'

We applaud as the violinist steps out onto the stage and accepts her award with a flushed face.

'Now, the runner-up,' the Dean continues. 'Congratulations Jordan Templeton for his piece, *Hometown*.'

'Oh my god,' I blurt before I can help myself. Jordan steps onto the stage and takes the award, shaking the Dean's hand. He looks down at the small trophy, as if he can't believe he's really holding it. Someone takes a photo, the light catches my eye. Briefly, I wonder if his dad will hear of this.

'Finally, the winner of the South Melbourne School of Arts Composition Prize is...,' he pauses for dramatic effect. 'Angus Chen for *Golden Nights in Shanghai*.'

The flutist emerges from the side of the stage and bows to the audience. He accepts his award from the Dean and then the entire group is directed to cram in for a on stage. The audience disperses. As we make our way to the foyer, Poppy pipes up. 'He didn't win?'

'He came second, Pops,' I correct. 'It's a really good effort.'

She thinks it over as we move towards the foyer. 'But he didn't win.'

'Sometimes it's not about winning,' I say. 'It's about doing what you love and giving things a go. No matter if you win or lose.'

I let her mull over it as Erin and I step into the foyer. 'Should we hang around?' Erin asks. 'We should, shouldn't we?'

I check my watch. It's only eight-thirty. 'It'd be nice to see him. Offer our congratulations. It was a big thing for him.'

'He'll be off to Los Angeles next,' Erin grins.

'Probably,' I say. We're barely a couple, yet I linger on the thought more than I should. Change the subject. 'You doing anything tomorrow?'

'Nothing,' Erin replies. For a moment, I think she looks cagey, like she's hiding something, but then Jordan emerges from the concert hall, and we lock eyes.

'Hey!' his face lights up as he sees me, and I love it. Love the way he looks at me like I'm the centre of his universe. 'You stayed!'

'We did,' Erin replies as she steps forward and gives him a hug. 'Congratulations. Second place!'

'Thank you,' he says and then leans forwards to hug me.

'It was a lovely piece,' I say, kissing him on the cheek. 'Congratulations.'

'Thank you.' He turns his attention to Poppy. 'I can't believe they didn't give out prizes for best dressed tonight because you certainly would have won.'

Poppy laughs and fluffs her tutu.

'Can you believe she picked it out all by herself?' Erin says, placing her hand on Poppy's head. 'Aspiring fashionista.'

'How much pink can one girl own?' Jordan says, catching on the joke.

'Never enough,' I reply. 'So is your phone ringing hot?'

'I'm honestly too scared to check it,' he replies. 'I just know Dad's gonna hear about this.'

Erin looks at me, and then down to Poppy. 'Well, kiddo, I think I saw a frozen yoghurt shop on the other side of the street. You feel like some?'

'Yeah!' Poppy nods.

Erin picks up Poppy and hitches her on her hip. 'We'll be over at the FroYo shop. Come by when you're done talking.'

I smile. Erin's hyper-sensitivity to people's cues finally pays off in my favour, and to prove a point, just as I'm about to say 'sugar-free FroYo only', Erin intercepts me. 'I know, sugar-free only.'

With that, Erin and Poppy head out into the street and leave Jordan and me in the quiet foyer. I take the award from him and turn it over in my hand. It's heavier than I thought: A treble cleft on a sturdy glass base. Immediately, I think it would make a great weapon for a fictional murderer.

'Thanks for coming,' he says. 'And sorry again for running out on you this morning.'

I hand the award back to him. 'It's fine. I'm glad you stayed last night.'

'Me too.' His hand reaches out and finds mine. 'You wanna go grab FroYo?'

A few of the other musicians are hanging around the foyer, chatting with various people I don't recognise but assume are important. 'You don't want to stay and network?'

'I've networked all my life, Ana,' he huffs, looking

around the room. 'They know who I am. Let's get FroYo.'

'You're sure?'

'One-hundred-and-ten percent,' he says and to either persuade me of his certainty, or to avoid further protests, he kisses me.

EPILOGUE

Mel stands beside me, nervousness clear on her face as she looks at the large block of decrepit townhouses. 'You really think you can save this place?'

During my first site visit to Holloway Houses, I'd left convinced that Erin and I had made a huge mistake and that we'd be paying for it for years to come. We couldn't offer housing. What a stupidly ambitious thing for us to undertake.

But now, a single townhouse stands stark against a block full of concrete shells and scaffolding. Six months ago, we signed the contract to buy. Now we've just finished restoring the first townhouse.

'That's the plan. Once they refurbish the other townhouses, we'll start offering them as needed to our client base.' I hold up a key. 'I thought you might like first pick.'

Mel stares at the key like it's a foreign item. 'What?'

'The first townhouse is finished. You can move in,' I say. 'There will be a bit of construction noise, but it's got lawn in the backyard and the toilet flushes. It's good to go.'

She takes the key from me and looks back at the townhouse. 'You're joking? Tell me you're joking.'

This is the best part of the job. 'Not joking.'

'And I can stay here?'

'For as long as you want,' I reply.

'Feels like we should have a bottle of champagne or something,' Mel says as she twists the key in the lock and opens the door to her new home. 'Oh my God, it's beautiful.'

The builders we've contracted have done a wonderful job. The refurbished windows stream light into the open living and entry space. I follow Mel as she walks into the kitchen, running her hand over the bench top.

'Upstairs are two bedrooms and a bathroom. The railings are all child-safe, and the builders will install the safety gate before you move in.' I open the sliding door to the backyard. 'The grass will take a few weeks to settle, but you've got space on the back wall to grow vegetables.'

'I'm literally lost for words,' Mel says as she steps onto the deck. I can hear the emotion in her voice; the way it wavers and catches as she speaks. 'I can't believe you've done this.'

'It's a team effort,' I reply. 'And if I'm being truthful, you kicked it all off. You and bloody Greg Pryor.'

That makes her laugh. 'I'm sure he'd be thrilled to know that.'

My smart watch vibrates, and I glance down at the message. It's from Erin: Meeting in 15! Shit.

'I'm so sorry, Mel, I've got to go,' I say. 'Just lock up

when you leave and Olivia will email you to arrange move-in dates and contracts.'

'Oh sure,' Mel says, her head popping out of the laundry cupboard.

Leaving Mel, I fish my car keys from my handbag. I'll be cutting it fine to get back to the office in fifteen minutes. Grabbing my phone, I message Erin back: *Stall them!*

Will try, she replies. *Also, your boyfriend delivered coffees. Cherish him, for he provides.*

Laughing at her message, I pull open the door to my Mercedes and toss my handbag on the front seat. My watch chimes again, but I ignore it. A moment later, Rafael's name flashes up on the dashboard screen, my phone pushing through the call via Bluetooth.

Raf never calls me.

I answer it. 'Hey Raf, I'm on a tight schedule. Is it urgent?'

'Yes,' he replies. 'It is.'

ACKNOWLEDGMENTS

I wrote this novel from July to November 2021, mostly in lockdown.

I think it takes a brave writer to admit that some books are hard to write. *The Next Big Thing* was that book for me; it is one of the most challenging books I've ever written.

In August 2021, a second, but necessary, lockdown in Canberra hit me harder than expected, and the crappy parts of life got in the way. Sitting down to spend time with Ana and Jordan, and the vibrant and dynamic community of south Melbourne, while stuck in my tiny apartment was often too much.

With that, I'd like to firstly thank my patient editor, Tegan Lyon. You took this manuscript, asked hard questions and made it better. Thank you for your guiding hand. Thanks for seeing the potential in the manuscript even when I felt lost.

Additionally, thank you to close friends Rebecca Cocks and Clair McDonald for their encouragement and support while writing. I'd like to thank my writing group, critique partners and, of course, my readers. The community we have made is so special to me. Thank you.

Finally, as Snoop Dogg so aptly put it: I wanna thank me.

ALSO BY ABRA PRESSLER

A feel-good Australian romance about food, community and first love nestled in the suburbs of Canberra, Australia.

Aspiring chef Luciano Jilani dreams of reopening his late mother's restaurant, but as a takeaway delivery driver, he's barely making ends meet.

Anse Meyer is a diplomat and an abysmal cook, relying on takeaway and frozen meals as he struggles with the demands of his 'dream job'.

When they meet via the delivery app, it's an awkward encounter with a handsome stranger. But then it happens again. And again. Craving more, Luciano offers to teach Anse how to cook. As they make their way through Luciano's mother's recipes, fledging friendship blooms into a consuming romance.

Read the first chapter of More in the back of the book!

CHAPTER 1

It's one day after the funeral, three days since his mother passed, only the sixth of January, and Luciano Jilani is just trying to get a cup of coffee without anyone recognising him. Or giving him their condolences. Or asking if there is anything, he, or his sisters, need.

Yes, there is one thing he needs: a bloody strong coffee.

With the funeral arrangements, the will, and the restaurant, he's barely had time to eat, shit, or sleep. Hopefully, the coffee will help to meet two of those needs while prolonging the third.

His sisters have been steadfast and level-headed throughout the entire process and frankly, he is in awe of them. There is so much to organise, so much to decide. Corina chose the dress she was cremated in, Marzia helped pick out the rose colour—*fuchsia*—and organised catering at the wake. He'd helped where he could. At the funeral service, they'd held his trembling hands, rubbed his shoulder, and he'd just *sat there,* barely able to process any of it until the Father had invited him to speak.

God, he needs a coffee.

Leafy oak trees line the busy street, smattering shade on the café tables across the road. A bell rings as Luciano steps out onto the road. There's barely a second to process the whiz of the bike before it zoom past him. Luciano presses his body against the side of the car, feels his sunglasses fall from his face and they crush under the bicycle's front tyre.

'Watch it, dickhead!' the cyclist barks. A *QIK-EATS* food pack bounces on the back of his bike.

'You watch it!' Luciano calls back and instantly regrets it. Both because his comebacks are always so lame, and because now all eyes are on him, and this entire situation is just a newspaper headline waiting to happen.

Luciano Jilani rages at local delivery driver days after mother's death!

It's not like he's unrecognisable: his face has been featured in at least six national newspapers and shared across social media in the days since his mother's funeral. He's tall and lanky, with olive skin and a head of chestnut hair that tends to have a distinctly Leo Sayer look if he lets it grow.

Everyone knows him in this town.

With sweaty palms, he fumbles open the car door before cranking the air conditioner up full blast. Cold air chills his sweat soaked skin. The car starts up with a purr.

༄

'Ugh, drive-thru coffee? Really?' Marzia groans as

Luciano balances three coffees and fights with the rusted fly screen door.

'The other place was closed.' It's a lie but Marzia doesn't press him on it. She takes her coffee and disappears back into the kitchen.

Corina eyes him suspiciously. 'You okay?

Luciano shrugs and sips his coffee. It's dull and mellow. 'I almost got mowed down by a dickhead on a delivery bike.'

'Did he scratch the car?' calls Marzia.

'No, I protected it with my body, thanks for your concern, Mar. He crushed my sunnies, though.'

Corina's writing thank you cards: to the funeral home, the minister's office, the local restaurants, business people, even the local radio station who reached out to help fund treatment. It had been in vain though: the chemo and radiation hadn't worked, and there was no way to operate. Still, the cards are a kind gesture. One Luciano is sure he would have forgotten. She hands him a stack. 'These are ready to go to the post if you want.'

It's mundane job, but at least it'll keep him busy.

Marzia is on the phone to a client when he arrives home, hot and sweaty, and Corina suggests that they get Chinese for dinner. Marzia hears this and pauses her phone call to snap, 'Not in my car, you're not', before unmuting the phone and continuing the conversation.

They take Corina's old Toyota Corolla to the Mr Long's Chinese restaurant, their well-loved local eatery.

'Did he ask about Mum?' says Luciano as she comes back to the car.

'Yeah.'

'I can't go anywhere without someone asking about her.'

'They miss her, Luc.' She starts up the car to get the air conditioner going again. 'It'll get better. You want to go for a drive?'

Luciano shrugs. It's better than sitting in the carpark with the car door half cracked, sweating in the heavy heat of the day.

They drive up the narrow leafy streets of Narrabundah and Luciano presses his forehead to the glass. Wordlessly, Corina turns towards Red Hill. The car splutters as it climbs the narrow road to the lookout.

'Why'd you bring us here?' Luciano inhales. The air is damp and heavy with the scent eucalyptus. Below them, Canberra glows red from the dying light of the sun. There are so many memories of her in this city, he is overwhelmed as they come rushing back.

'Did you see Rohan at the funeral yesterday?' Corina pulls her long, curly hair off her shoulders and into a messy bun. 'Marzia said he was sitting near the back of the church.'

'The whole thing was a bit of a blur,' Luciano admits. He barely remembers anyone at the funeral, except his sisters and the pastor, the muskiness of the church and the rigidity of the pews against his spine. 'Why is he back?'

'Apparently he got kicked out of his footy club. Guess he's moved back here now.'

'Did you talk to him at the wake?'

'Didn't see him.'

'I haven't seen his dad since we closed the restaurant. Speaking of, I should go suss out the damage tomorrow.'

'You don't have to,' Corina says. 'Take it slowly.'

Luciano kicks a rock. It skids across the road and tumbles down the embankment. 'How slowly, though? Shouldn't I be trying to get things back to normal?'

'Things won't go back to normal,' replies Corina. 'But if you want to go tomorrow, I'll come with you.'

He wants to tell her he'd prefer to go by himself; to work through things without an audience but her phone vibrates and then she's stepping away from him. The moment's gone.

'Come on.' She unlocks the car. 'Dinner's ready.'

The rich aroma of honey chicken fills the and the takeaway containers seep warmth through Luciano's shorts. By the time they get back to the house, they've broken into the complimentary bag of prawn crackers.

Marzia is hunched over the dining table, thumbing through documents again. A half-empty mug of cold tea sits beside her.

'Food's hot.' Luciano grabs the wine glasses from the kitchen cupboard. 'C'mon, Mar, come eat.'

She waves him off. 'In a bit. I'm just working through a few things.'

Luciano spies the bank's logo on the header of a document and decides not to press it.

The cricket's on TV. It's not something Luciano would usually watch, but Corina's big on sports and he doesn't feel like bickering with her. There's a calmness to it: the monotonous voice of the commentator, the rhythmic cycle of the game.

Eventually, Marzia comes over to them, dressed in a pair of cotton shorts and one of Luciano's hoodies she's flogged without permission.

'Can we watch something else?' Marzia demands as she sits crossed-legged on the floor.

'No,' says Corina.

Luciano nudges Marzia's shoulder with his toes. 'Corina said you saw Rohan at the funeral?'

'Yeah,' Marzia mutters through a mouthful of Mongolian lamb. 'Omala too. He's moved back in with his parents again. Stopped playing footy.'

'Why?' Luciano asks.

'Didn't say.'

'I heard he hit the clubs a little too hard,' Corina says. 'Got involved in some stuff he shouldn't.'

That doesn't really sound like Rohan, but it has been a few years since they've seen each other.

'I don't even go for the Tigers, but I seemed to have watched a lot of their games last year,' Corina continues. 'There was one game where he literally had his shirt ripped off and-,'

'All right, I'm done.' Luciano steps over Marzia's shoulder awkwardly. 'I won't be a part of this conversation.'

'How is this not something you want to talk about?' Marzia sniggers as she takes his place on the lounge. 'The man's a beefcake.'

'No one says beefcake, Marzia,' Luciano groans. 'I'm showering.'

'Cold showering, maybe,' Corina retorts.

Luciano closes the bathroom door to the sound of Marzia's laughter. It's nice. He doesn't remember the last time he heard laughter in this house. The sounds of machines whirling had become too commonplace.

They're still talking when he cracks the bathroom door open fifteen minutes later. Grabbing the bottles from the shower, he's about to ask if Corina wants their mother's curly-haired shampoo and conditioner when he hears Marzia say, 'We have to tell him, Corina.'

'There has to be something we can do. Move a few things around?'

There's a pause. He stays in the shadows of the hall-way, listening.

'I've tried. This is the only option.'

'It'll destroy him.'

Marzia releases a painful sigh. 'I know.'

Keep reading *More* by downloading or purchasing from your preferred retailer:

Amazon

Kobo

Barnes and Noble

Other major retailers.

ABOUT THE AUTHOR

Abra Pressler grew up in rural NSW and currently lives in Canberra, Australia. She's been writing since she was thirteen and holds a Bachelor of Arts (Creative Writing) from RMIT University where she wrote her graduating thesis on romantic comedies.

When she's not writing, Abra enjoys coffee, bushwalking and consuming every cinnamon roll that's ever existed.

The Next Big Thing is her second novel and the first in the Woods Sisters series.

Want more?

Join my incredible community! Instagram is my shit, so please feel free to connect with me there.

Sign up to receive news on latest releases from the author on www.abrapressler.com.